Y0-BTU-325

WATCH OUT

by

Joseph Suglia

Copyright © 2006 by Joseph Suglia
ISBN 1-891855-77-8

This book is a work of fiction. Names, characters, places,
situations and incidents are the product of the author's
imagination or are used fictitiously. Any resemblance to actual
events, locales, or persons, living or dead, is purely coincidental.
All rights reserved, including the right of reproduction in whole or
in part in any form.

Published in the United States
FLF Press
PO Box 711612
Herndon VA 20171
Printed in the United States

Many thanks to graphic artist John Nail for the cover design.
Mr. Nail may be reached at: tojonail@bellsouth.net.

Book and text design by Milton Stern. Mr. Stern can be
reached at milton@FLF.org

Thanks — Melinda Dye, Ben Edelberg, Krissy Getman, Danny Gallegos, Peter Lambert, Rob Rana, Domenic, Domenic, Jr., and Rob Rossi.

Thanks — Eric Plattner, the ideal reader.

Thanks — Antonin Artaud, Pierre Klossowski, Alain Robbe-Grillet, and Boris Vian.

WATCH OUT

by

Joseph Suglia

Those young girls who surround the animal cages in zoos cannot help but be amazed by the ever-so lubricious rear ends of apes.

— Georges Bataille

This novel is rated X. It contains scenes of nudity, sexuality, and violence, as well as adult themes and offensive language.
Parental guidance is strongly advised.

Contents

I

Immobility

Suddenly, my body loses its ability to move.
There is nothing to do.
I accept — and even enjoy — my paralysis.
I wrap silence around myself and explore my most intimate recesses.
Hidden roads lead to secret cities.
Though outside of the classroom is a riot of activity, here I am at an infinite remove from the events of the world.
I examine the contours of my mind without interruption.
I ball myself up in the hollow of a womb.
No one touches me anymore.
I feel the moist breath of midnight against my neck.
The night, it is invigorating.
A balmy, nocturnal wind traverses these empty spaces.
The wind is my creature.
I observe the shapes of the night with nyctalopian pupils.
Through the open window, I see the circling nightbirds.
How the nightbirds sway and swing in the air.
How they disappear into the vastitude of space.
The nightbirds are my creatures.
Now I am dissolving in the darkness.
Erase my outline.
My form deliquesces.
My head melts like a loaf of chocolate mousse on a sweltering summer's day.
See my eyeholes widen.
My body fluidifies.

Joseph Suglia

The surrounding atmosphere tightens around my skeletonized form like a transparent sheet.

A whirl of black envelops me.

I cast my mind into the abyss.

I am immersed in the weltering night.

The darkness deepens and thickens.

But from where I am lying, the core of darkness isn't dark enough.

I am the Him

I hope that this train explodes into flames.

I've been in this hot metal chamber for six hours. I'm sitting on the upper level. No one had better sit next to Me. Or talk to Me. I loathe humanity. Look at those insects! Squirming vermin! A woman sticks her lactating nipple into a baby's pink mouth. Cover yourself up, she-freak! Two lovers massage each other's lips with their tongues. Nothing is worse than that. Open expressions of desire. They're like mongooses in rut. *A spasm of revulsion wells up inside of Me, an overflowing current of disgust.* Leave Me be. Traveling by train is treacherous. You have to deal with the mob. Average people disgust Me. I should have rented a car.

The train rattles like a psychotic vibrator.

I stare out the window. A steady parade of objects enters My thought-vision. A radio antenna blossoming into the sky like a giant turkey baster. A fat corn silo. A barn. A windmill. A hemorrhaging river. A wooden bridge. A billboard advertising chicken-powdered French fries. These things stream past. I cannot hold them in My sight. It almost seems as if everything that is happening outside were a reflection of the film that is endlessly spooling inside My mind.

All of these things belong to Me. Nature is My property.

When will the train arrive in Benton Harbor, Michigan? I want out. Trains are like prisons. You can't get away from them. They're everywhere. The mob. They speak to you. They grab you. They look at you. I hate all of these grandmotherfuckers. If only the

world were vacant of human life. I'm the only real egoist. Everyone is concerned for himself. We're all self-seeking. We are all trapped in the deserts of our solitude. But I'm the only one whose life matters.

I unstick and raise Myself. Need to wolf down something warm. I've gone completely luncheonless for six hours. I can't imagine what grub they're hawking on this train. *Wo Mir die Welt in den Weg kommt — und sie kommt Mir immer in den Weg — da verschlinge Ich sie, um meinen Hunger nach Herrschaft zu stillen.* Gripping the railing, I descend the metallic staircase that leads to the lower level. Where is the diner car? I have no choice. Get back. Stay away from Me. The mindless horde. The senseless rabble.

As I reach the bottom of the stairwell, the train climaxes. I fall forward, thrusting My head against the wall. Fuck it. Here they come. A torrent of passengers funnels into the aisles. With aching slowness, an old man trembles past Me, his cadaverous body creeping toward the exit.

I hiss through My teeth, "Move it, Mister Liver Spots!"

The throng begins to empty the train. I enter the swarm, trying to avoid physical contact. They probe Me with inquisitive eyes. Let no one touch Me. They always try to touch Me. A thick stench of humanity fills My nostrils. I balk and coil at the touch of a disgustingly oversized middle-aged woman. Her fat talons fasten onto My right arm for support. Recoiling, I squeal with nausea. My body shrivels and shrinks. She would look like Jabba the Hut, if Jabba the Hut wore waxy lip gloss. Must get out. Get out of here.

I break into a clearing. The teeming mass is behind Me now. Leave Me be. Human rot. I scramble hurriedly toward the diner car, My suitcase dangling from My

clenched fingers. Corpse-rot. Dead matter. They are all compost, slag dead matter.

Dear Me, I was rude, was I not? You want to know who I am and what I am doing.

Who am I, then?

I am Jonathan Barrows.

Let Me begin again.

This name, "Jonathan Barrows," only vaguely approximates who I really am.

Who am I, then?

I am the Him.

The absolute being.

Understand that I am not merely one being among other beings. I am *the* being, the being of all beings.

Where is the diner car? As I pass them, they look up at Me admiringly. They can sense My supreme greatness. They know, they pre-know, that I am like no one else. I am the highest form that humanity has reached. Indeed, I am, without doubt, the most extraordinary being who has ever existed. I stride into the diner car. All of these fools. Noisome sheep. They are nothing more than props on My stage. Tools, I can use them how I please. I have never met a single human being who is on My level. The history of humanity is nothing more than a preparation for My emergence into the world.

The diner car resembles a cloister.

In relation to Me, human beings are beastly beasts. Even to use the term, "relation" is misleading, since there is no relationship whatsoever between Me and what passes for "humanity." Human beings are such miserable creatures, unworthy of dwelling in My presence. The world belongs to Me and to Me alone. All of these fools! They are misbirths, abortions, mistakes.

Humankind is a cosmic error. My existence is alone significant. Why the fuck are they here?

The train rockets past a swamp, unslumbering the moorfowl.

I have a mind quicker than a cheetah. They cannot reach the reaches of My greatness. My intelligence is unsurpassed. For this reason, they hate Me. If I were to die? Their lives would have no meaning. My dissertation "advisor" hated Me as intensely as the slave hates the plantation owner. Because I towered over him. He desired to become Me, like everyone else, and therefore despised Me. I made him feel his own insignificance. *Ils Me méprisent parce que Je suis Monsieur Parfait.* He wrote a letter of condemnation on My behalf in which he stated, "Jonathan Barrows is too serious to teach anyone German philosophy." Revenge of the feeble.

The train vibrates like a sociopathic electric dildo.

As a result, I was blackballed. I applied in vain for professorial positions at prestigious universities throughout the country. Benton Harbor Community College is the only college that would grant Me an interview. For this reason, I am on a train to Benton Harbor, Michigan, where My interview will take place.

I purchase a freeze-dried egg sandwich, mummified in cellophane. I unravel the wrapper.

The most noble of men is traveling to the most ignoble of cities.
The university belongs to Me.

Benton Harbor has a well-deserved inferiority complex. Read the travel guide. It is known only for the poverty of its residents and occasional murders and outbreaks of unrest. There is absolutely no reason to recommend the city to anyone.

Some of you may be wondering why I would accept an interview to teach in such a city.

A star needs a dark background in order to shine.

I am unblemished by the taint of human scum.

The freeze-dried egg sandwich lies unwrapped in My limber hands. The train jets through a cornfield. See the cornstalks undulating in the wind. Corn — the most vital staple of nutrition in the United States. Corn — increasingly in demand and never-ending in supply. The cornfield is a paradise for senior citizens throughout the nation.

Breezing past My sight are husks upon husks of water-glistened corn-tomatoes, genetic mutations born from the hybridization of tomatoes and corn.

A mucous-stained boy shifts into My line of vision. He sits opposite Me, wearing his official *Fight Club* T-shirt.

Look at that port-wine stain on his forehead! How repulsive!

The gossoon wants to speak with Me.

He gazes at Me with undisguised veneration.

He peruses Me through the low slants of his eyelashes.

Like a starving street urchin, he yearns to pluck peaches from the trees that grow in My forest.

He hungers for My flesh.

That hunger will remain forever unsatisfied.

I yawn and settle back in My chair, studying the outlines of My reflection in the window.

The Unmanned Station

The wind is wild.

It whirls around and whips My legs.

The train has departed. With suitcase in hand, I scan the parking lot for automobiles. Behind Me, the waves clap hands.

Casting My eyes back and forth, I wander through the belly of this vast, dark space. No one is here. An emissary from the community college was supposed to have retrieved Me at the train station.

He has not come.

The station is unmanned.

Vapor rises through the sewer grates, a thick shower in reverse.

Above Me floats a tall wooden staircase.

I ascend the staircase, fastening My sight on the climb.

Across a stretch of tar looms the Crystalline Hotel.

I traverse the wide space, moving toward the hotel, My suitcase clattering behind Me.

I tug My suitcase through the door of the Crystalline Hotel.

The lobby is un-peopled except for the desk clerk.

Despite the fact that he is a dumpy pygmy with a long, brown ponytail, the desk clerk bears a certain resemblance to David Bowie.

I say with affected nonchalance, "I'd like a room."

He replies, "We, like, only have one room left. Like, I swear to God. And it's, like, not even air-conditioned."

It is an unusually hot summer.

I ask him, "Why isn't the room air-conditioned?"

"The air conditioning is, like, down and shit."

"If it is the only room available, I'll resign Myself to that fact."

"So you want it?"

"Yes, I'll take the room."

"What's your name?"

"My name is Jonathan Barrows. J-O-N-A-T-H-A-N B-A-R-R-O-W-S."

"That is such a cool name."

"Yes," I say, "I know."

The desk clerk chortles joylessly.

"Do you, like, wanna pay cash or by check or by credit card?"

"I have a Visa."

I slap the plastic card on the counter.

"Do you have an ID?"

I place My driver's license on the counter.

The desk clerk studies My driver's license with frenzied curiosity.

Glimmering with surprise, his face suddenly bursts into a smile, as if he noticed something for the first time, something that could redeem his life and make it meaningful.

I have seen this expression many times on many different faces.

Looking up from My driver's license, the porter speaks, the words rapidly flowing from his bent mouth.

"Look, I'm not, like, gay or anything, but I think that we have a lot in common and stuff. I mean, we're about the same age and, I mean, it gets kinda lonely in this hotel when you're all by yourself. Maybe we could play Uno or something or get a bite to eat at Lobster King. It's right down the street, did you see it? On Impression Avenue. I've got some coupons for a free meal at Lobster King. You buy one meal, and the next one doesn't cost anything, as long as you order the shrimp basket. Maybe, if you want, you can sleep at

my place. It's right down the hall. I know that you like air conditioning and stuff, and it can get kinda hot at night, since now it's, like, the summer. I've got air conditioning and a cot. You can sleep on the cot. Or, like, if you want, I could, like, sleep on the cot, and you could sleep on the bed."

"Are there any other hotels in the area?"

"No, like, this is the only one in Benton Harbor. The other ones are infested with big-ass black beetles. Dude, I'm totally serious. The black beetles, they're, like, *huge*."

The desk clerk stares at Me moistly.

I insist upon a solitary room. I tell the desk clerk that I'll be staying for two nights, but I suspect that it might be longer.

After receiving confirmation from My bank, the desk clerk proffers Me a key, which is shaped like a wooden fish.

His face distorted with fatigue, the desk clerk says, "I'm gonna be here, like, the whole fucking night, dude, and if you want to talk or watch TV, just come down and let me know, OK?"

The desk clerk requires My acknowledgment.

He knows — whether "consciously" or "unconsciously" — that he does not exist outside of My recognition.

Training My suitcase, I walk away in silence.

I tow My freight into the elevator.

The elevator hums as it ascends.

Is silence a form of communication, or is communication a form of silence?

The Prince saunters through the corridors of the hotel, cradling a soft dove in His arms.
The heart of the dove pulses warmly.
The dove is a mechanical object.

I slip the key into the door and twist it until the lock snaps.

Amour propre

Once when I was in graduate school, after spending the day reading Joris-Karl Huysmans's *En Rade*, I turned on the television set in My atelier and watched a few minutes of an Argentinian film that featured a woman showering *completely naked*.

I was, of course, horrified. Slippery gorgon. My insides contorted with disgust, I rushed across the room and kicked the cathode ray tube until it hissed. Despite the violent reaction that it provoked within Me, that film had a salubrious impact upon My life.

The next day, after giving a seminar presentation that would alter the lives of all those present, I set up a video camera in front of My private shower, undid the curtain, and filmed Myself showering.

I value that recording. One can see spume streaming through the chasm of My plump buttocks. One can see beads of water glistening on My taut stomach. One can see the heaving of My beautiful chest. The video, which I've entitled *My Shower*, is the most striking film ever made.

While I shower in My hotel room, I imagine watching Myself shower on television. There should be a video screen in here. Also a computer with Internet access.

If only I could dispatch this image throughout the globe.

Images of Me showering. There is nothing more breathtaking. There is nothing more beautiful than this beautiful vision.

Like a deer, I prance gracefully out of My shower stall. In the privacy of this silent interior, I spin and whirl.

I do not cake My body with powdery substances. I do not douse Myself with sweet unguents. I do not

spray My body with exotic perfumes. I exude a musty musk that draws both women and men into My sphere. My sweet-smelling reek prompts everyone within a two-mile radius to betray his most intimate desires.

Their desires are always the same. They want the electricity that flows from My body to enter their own. They want to nuzzle their muzzles against My warm flesh.

Hot damn, I am a fascinating man — a stiffening, rigidifying, mesmerizing man.

Both women and men are attracted to Me in the way that flies are attracted to filet mignon.
— Jonathan Barrows

Too bad for them. I do not know the dubious joys of fellow-feeling. I have no need for companionship. I am inclined toward no one.

It is often said that women are the paragons of beauty. This statement is not merely incomprehensible. It is self-contradictory. A woman can no more be beautiful than the sun can rotate around the earth.

I do not find women appealing. In fact, they nauseate Me. Women are the paragons of the disgusting.

When I was a teaching assistant, an allegedly "attractive" young female student approached Me after a discussion session. I think that her name was "Nicole" or "Nancy" or "Natalia" or something along those lines.

Her name definitely started with the letter, "N."

Gazing up at Me with adoration, she said, "Johnny you're so smart. I'd really like to talk with you. Can we

meet sometime soon? I want to talk about the things that you said in class. We can meet for drinks real casual."

During our ill-starred meeting at the local coffee shop, N. remarked in a hushed voice, "I'll give you everything. I'll let you do whatever you want."

She then whispered, "My body is *yours*."

"I appreciate your candor, N.," I said patiently and slowly. "Certainly, you have good taste. I am indeed the pinnacle of magnificence. To presume that I would deign to touch you, however, is the height of effrontery. Your impertinence, indeed, goes beyond all limits. How could you imagine that someone of My caliber would agree to touch someone as lowly as you? You are no more important to Me than an amoeba or a slimy tadpole. Like all women, you are an inferior life form."

N.'s mouth spread open wide. Her eyes threatened to spill out of her skull and into her well-deep double mocha espresso latte.

"Why don't you like girls."

Unsure of whether this was a question or a statement, I said without looking at her, "There are multiple reasons why women are inherently disgusting creatures, N. I will enumerate them.

"Ovulation, first of all. You menstruate. This is a sign that you are essentially incomplete. Flows of blood flood your vaginal folds. Indeed, your valves never cease to bleed. Why would I want to touch a thing that bleeds? I have no desire to drown in the menstrual flood."

Menopause is good; it should be welcomed and affirmed.
— Jonathan Barrows

Joseph Suglia

"Secondly, the female genitals. The mons pubis is absurdly grotesque, with all of its nodes and lobes. What sickening excrescences! Your labia are sloppy things. What could be more revolting than the vaginal schism? And the way that you creatures smell! Vaginal mucous stenches. I would rather have sexual intercourse with a squid than insert My penis into the hollow of a vagina.

"Women are such peculiarly formed creatures, with your mammillated chests and bulging anuses. Breasts are strange. Such odd fleshy protrusions! Your cantilevered mounds of adipose tissue! They are often blue-membraned and downed with fuzz. And the way that they jiggle! The uneasy way that mammae quiver makes Me queasy.

"Your papules are like helpless pink-purple eyes, stupidly staring at nothing. Weird conical things! Nothing — absolutely nothing! — is more grotesque than papillary hair.

"When women age, their breasts transform into wizened milkless udders."

N. looked at Me through tear-red eye-slits. She convulsed vehemently.

"You're gay," she said between sobs. "Why don't you just say that you're gay?"

"I am sorry to disappoint you, N.," I said, "but I am not gay. I simply don't find you attractive."

Her face reddened and worn, she screamed, "Go ahead call me a fish you fucking faggot!"

The café-goers lifted their heads from their steamy cappuccinos.

"To a certain extent," I said unperturbed, "your drawn features and protuberant teeth do resemble

18

those of a piranha. I wouldn't quite put you in the 'fish' category, however.

"Your teeth may also be likened to dominoes."

"YOURE GAY! YOURE GAY! YOURE GAY!"

N. said this, of course, to balm the wound of rejection.

She was incorrect. I was not — and certainly am not — a homosexual.

Nor am I merely a misogynist. Men repel Me, as well. My androphobia, in fact, knows no limits.

Even though I have, from a purely external point of view, male genitalia, the sight of a penis fills Me with even more disgust than the sight of a gaping vaginal canal.

Men are more nauseating than women.
— Jonathan Barrows

When I was at "Sepp" Herberger High School, a male student — I think that his name was Dirk Owen or Owen Davis — swayed toward Me across the locker room and unveiled his male genital organ.

Yee-hah.

The organ looked at Me slipperily.

Dirk Owen propositioned Me playfully while prodding his purple-veined protuberance.

I quickly rebuffed his advances.

I said without looking at him, "No, Dirk, I will not touch you. Nothing could be more sickening than the body of a man. I detest the swell of the male paunch. Sagging testes sicken Me. Worse still, your buttocks are often hairy. If men want to appear less repulsive, then they should shave their hairy buttocks. I disapprove of hair. At least women depilate. For that

reason alone, women are less hideously unpleasant than men."

Dirk Owen's eyes moistened and then bubbled over with fresh tears.

Wailing like a harpooned dog, Dirk Owen fled the locker room.

No one appeals to Me sexually. Give Me a full-body condom, and I'll be happy. I want a prophylactic shield that would screen Me from all human contact.

Envelop Me in a cone of vellum.

Nonetheless, I do not suffer from *anaesthesia sexualis*. I do know sexual desire.

I am an auto-sexual. That is: I am sexually attracted to Myself and to no one else.

"Why?" you ask.

Why? Because I am lovely. I am, in fact, an impossibly beautiful man.

Beauty is an illusion — except in My case.

I am not merely the standard by which all things beautiful are measured. I am the only instance of beauty in an otherwise ridiculously ugly world. In relation to Me, everyone and everything is ghastly in appearance.

"Relation" may not be the word.

Dear God or whomever, I am gorgeous.

I have clear blue eyes and wavy blonde hair.

My face glows. It is Olympian in its splendor.

And My body? No one has a physique as exquisite as Mine. Indeed, My form is cosmically perfect.

Gaze at My segmented abdomen.

My skin is as white as fresh mayonnaise.

My beautiful, beautiful buttocks spread apart and couple as I walk.

My bowel movements are vigorous and healthy.

The tentacles of My pubic hair extend everywhere like the fronds of a massively distending fern.

Hot damn, I am hot!

I am so beautiful that I excite Myself.

I caress My Nair-smoothed legs while moaning with deep pleasure.

A human erector set, I give Myself a luscious erection.

Yes, it is time to water My erotic garden. From the sanctuary of My bed, I reach into My suitcase and grasp a leather sheath. I open the sheath and remove a sheaf of photographs.

Wherever I go, images of My penis accompany Me.

One of My favorite images displays My penis turned on its side, its tip sleepily staring at the camera's viewfinder and smiling. Its ridged shaft and glans resemble the neck and head of a brontosaurus.

My penis is like a crossbow waiting to be fired into the abyss.

The aperture of My penis puckers like the mouth of a tiny fish.

Soma is spirit.

I touch My penis with delight while staring at the photograph of My penis. I cradle My testes in My hands, massaging them delicately and lovingly.

Yes, Professor Jonathan Barrows masturbates while staring at naked pictures of himself.

In the abysses of My solitude, I am My own Significant Other.

The photographs, although immensely appealing, do not succeed in bringing Me to orgasm. I must find another way of provoking My desires.

I read aloud My translation of Max Stirner's deliciously lubricious masterpiece, *The Unique Individual and Its Property,* while stroking My torso and devouring deshelled oyster guts from a formica bowl.

Listen!

My voice floats balletically through the hotel room.

Love never involves self-sacrifice. The idiot-culture in which I live commands Me to love "My fellow brothers and sisters." Like a drill sergeant, it orders Me to love "humankind."

Yes, let "us" all "love one another"!

The desk clerk loves Me because he wants to release his seminal fluids into My anus, My parents love Me because I am a thing that they can show off, and every other woman loves Me because she wants Me to press My penis into her vaginal canal.

Life is selfish.
Love is selfish.

I insert My right index finger into My anal orifice.

I slam the book's lid closed.

It is difficult to masturbate and study metaphysics at the same time.

The photographs don't work. Stirner doesn't work.

My adventures in auto-eroticism are always meticulously stage-managed.

I open My suitcase and draw out THE OFFICIAL JONATHAN BARROWS BLOW-UP DOLL. It is a nearly perfect replica of My body, customized and minutely detailed according to My precise specifications. It cost Me over two thousand dollars. I would have gladly paid twice that sum.

Downy hair blossoms in the gulfs of its armpits.

Downy hair blossoms in the gulfs of My armpits.

I rush to My private shower and run warm water over the inflatable love doll. I want its body to feel as warm and supple as My own.

With the doll flaccid and corrugated in My hands, I return to the bed. Reclining on the sheets like a drunken courtesan, I gaze at My double with reverence.

I spread out and smooth and stroke its rippled skin.

I purse My lips and clamp them onto its nozzle as if I were a suckling infant.

I draw My breath and breathe into the body of the clone, My dream lover.

Slowly inflating, the love doll resembles a human body decaying in reverse.

Its creases and crevices smooth and straighten.

Inhale, exhale, inhale, exhale.

It pulses to the rhythm of My respiration.

Its ears pop out. Its fingers extrude.

The penis of the undecomposing doll salutes Me.

Outside of Me, there is no Outside.
Nothing outside of Me has any meaning whatsoever.
The world exists only in order to be digested by Me.
I gourmandize everyone who gets in My way.
Your Church. Your school. Your society. Your workplace. Your cults. Your humanity.
All of these things are ties that will never bind My wrists.

I touch the clone, trailing My index finger around its well-aerated rubber areolae, astonished by their near-perfect verisimilitude.

I breathe darkly.

What craftsmanship!

Joseph Suglia

The halos that ring the doll's nipples are lusciously empurpled with factory dye.

As I suck and lick the doll's nipples and areolae, a few flakes of purple dye detach and adhere to My lips.

I am the transcendental self.

Foreplay has come to an end. I pull out a tube of lubricant from My suitcase. I squeeze the thick, gelatinous liquid into the doll's anal orifice.

I plunge into the doll's buttocks, which are identical to My own buttocks.

I devour the doll's phallus, which is identical to My own phallus.

I make love to My double.

I infuse the doll with sweet pleasure.

I infuse Myself with sweet pleasure.

Pleasure flows through the doll's veins.

Pleasure flows through My veins.

I have sexual intercourse with Myself.

Out of My penis surges a stream of warm semen.

Yowza yowza yowza yowza yowza yowza yowza yowza yowza yowza yowza yowza yowza yowza yowza yowza yowza yowza yowza!

The Interview Does Not Take Place

After gratifying Myself, I sleep steadily for nine hours. I wake up, shower, and dress Myself in the mirror with preening self-admiration. I walk stealthily from the Crystalline Hotel to the Benton Harbor Community College. It is Tuesday.

According to the e-mail that I received from Dr. Mendoza, the interview will take place at 1:30 pm today.

With the exception of Lake Michigan College, Benton Harbor Community College is the only post-secondary educational institution in Benton Harbor, Michigan. The entire college is housed in a single gray building that lies five miles south of Lake Michigan. Like most of the community colleges that were founded in American cities in the middle of the twentieth century, Benton Harbor Community College prides itself on an open admissions policy: literally anyone — including whores, bums, illiterates, half-wits, drunks, and convicted sex offenders — can gain admittance to this palace of knowledge.

As might be expected, the college resembles a sewer.

On the high ceilings dangle bile-colored tiles.

The walls of the classrooms are decorated with an indiscriminate yellow matter.

Middle-aged students shamble down the prison-like corridors, their eyes darkened from manic depression; most of them are loud-mouthed, overweight idiots. Others resemble truck drivers or construction workers; these students are pursuing a degree in refrigerator maintenance. Benton Harbor Community College is a sanctuary for future air-conditioning specialists.

A woman with blubbery lips muscles past Me, slobbers over herself, and shouts, "IM GOIN TO SCHOOL NOW TORI!"

Generous folds of fat drape her massive torso. Her adipose tissue wiggles as she waddles.

These people are unteachable. Their degrees are meaningless. Nonetheless, I will acquire a position here. I enjoy teaching. Squatting students, writing down what I say, spooning down every word.

I reel through the hallways.

The School of Learning is situated on the seventh floor of the college, next to a fast-food restaurant called "Burger God."

Burger God's emblem is a grinning surprised hamburger. Around the happy hamburger head spins a penumbral halo. Huddled around round tables, students gulp down duck nuggets with pomegranate or papaya sauce and ketchup-dipped chicken-powdered French fries.

I swing into the office of the School of Learning.

Blotches of syrupy excrement stain the walls. Heaps of unbound paper litter the floor.

Behind a partitioned desk is a woman with a mammoth beehive hairdo. She is alone in the office. She isn't doing anything except looking at Me.

She is like everyone else except she is like everyone else.

She is sitting in a big chair.

The chair is really, really, really big.

The woman stands up and thrusts her hand forward as if she wanted to clutch My throat and says in a voice raspy with gravel, "Sheila Grimmlager."

I extend My hand, dreading the inescapable moment when Miss Grimmlager's hand will touch My own.

Shaking the hand of the other person is an act of extreme self-abandonment.

Although, from a purely external point of view, I welcome her to touch My hand, this gesture is, at once, an invitation and the revocation of the same invitation. Her hand is a trap, a cat's cradle.

I release the throw; Miss Grimmlager catches it. She will palm My palm.

Her hand grazes My own. It feels like a hot water bottle or a glove bloated with bull semen. It clamps down on My fingers and compresses them, fondling the skin around My fingernails.

Miss Grimmlager pants. My hand retracts quickly, sliding out of her fingers as if it were an eel slipping through the interstices of a fishing trawl.

"Hello, Miss Grimmlager. I am Professor Jonathan Barrows. We've been trading e-mails over the past two weeks. I'm sure that you remember Me."

"Professor Barrows? No, I don't remember who you are."

"I'm here for the interview."

She stares at Me blankly.

I say with contrived meekness, "I'm a bit early, I know."

"I wasn't aware that there would be any interviews today. For what position did you apply?"

"Assistant Professor of Intelligent Thinking."

Like a librarian garbed in urine-moist panties, Miss Grimmlager squirms.

She says to My pristinely white teeth, "Dr. Mendoza conducts all of the interviews in the School of Learning. He'd be the one interviewing you. But he won't be coming in today."

My penis rigidifies.

The rigidification of My penis has nothing to do with Miss Grimmlager.

"When does he come to campus?"

She says to My luscious abdominal muscles, "He teaches a seminar every Monday. It's his only course this summer."

The words splashed in the trough of her mouth before they were expressed.

She did not answer the question that I posed to her.

"Monday at what time?"

She says to My perfectly shaped pelvis, "From six until nine, but sometimes, class adjourns later."

"In which room is the seminar held?"

She says to My protruding biceps, "Room 121."

"What is the name of the course, if I may ask?"

"'Loving Yourself, Loving Others, and Loving Me.'"

Heaving vigorously, Miss Grimmlager sits back down and straightens her back.

Hot damn, that chair is really big.

"Please ask Dr. Mendoza to telephone Me at the Crystalline Hotel, so we can instantiate an interview."

Miss Grimmlager jots down something on a yellow notepad.

"The Crystalline Hotel ... Jonathan Barrows. I'll tell him myself the next time that I see him, Professor Barrows."

Outside the window, the sun scribbles an indecipherable message on the palimpsest of the afternoon.

"Yes, please do," I say, gesturing vaguely. "Please tell him that I came for the interview and that I'd like to speak with him."

"I'll be happy to do so, Professor Barrows."

I worm out of the office and walk briskly down the corridor, My legs arcing gracefully through space. I stare with contempt at the mentally retarded students who shamble past Me.

It is difficult to use the verb, *to instantiate* and still sound smooth.

Ye Olde Diner

I sashay into a diner called "Ye Olde Diner." I would rather cut off My own ears with garden shears than enter such an establishment, but My digestive gland is clamoring for hot victuals.

I sit down at the most isolated table in the restaurant.

What a parade of circus freaks!

A solitary old man grazes over a bowl of artificial bacon flakes.

Coffee fog steams his spectacles.

His head turns interrogatively.

The glass glares at Me.

A bimbot clamps her teeth around a mashed egg sandwich while blathering with her repulsive girlfriends. They, the bimbots, stench of aquarium pebbles. The shopping mall is their village.

An ornate dish of gherkins is passed to receiving hands.

The waiter approaches Me, his lips smacking noisily. He resembles David Bowie, even though he has a bloated face, corrugated lips, lopsided eyes, an oversized nose, and a brow littered with unbandaged gashes.

He wears a necklace made out of corn kernels and a wasp-colored bracelet. As he flips open his notepad, I notice that the lips of his hands are nearly bleeding.

I peruse the menu.

Escargo coffee. Iowa salad — a plate of live slugs squirming over cabbage leaves — Oysters.

"I'll have the oysters."

The waiter looks at My lovely irises and says, "You know that oysters are an aphrodisiac. You know what

that word means, 'aphrodisiac.' It means that it makes people frisky. What I ..."

His voice trails off like a dying snail.

As he speaks, I listen to the sounds of My mind.

Men make Me want to regurgitate.

Without listening, I interrupt him and say, "And I'll also have an egg cream. You know how to make an egg cream, don't you?"

His face reddening, the waiter says pertly, "No, but I'm sure that Chef Wilson does."

Once he is out of sight, I walk uneasily toward the jukebox. Everyone in the diner watches Me through slanted eyelashes. I am the stud of studs.

Above the jukebox is an overwhelmingly complex painting.

Basilisks, gestated by hermaphroditic roosters, slink through the tunnels of a sewer system.

Verminous sewer-fiends scale the mazelike funnels and sluices.

A lunar owl's face drifting, sleepwalking, like an empty billowing caravan through the midnight air.

A cruciform tree towers into the sky.

Behind the tree is a crucifix made of still-bleeding deer carcasses.

Skinless deer prance across a darkened flax-field.

A venison marketer hawks deer-flesh.

A woman wrapped in gossamer husks of wheat sings an inaudible canticle.

Her frozen pink lips generate imperceptible sounds.

Umber-speckled cattle creep unspeedily through the waving flax.

Showers of gentle white blankets descend, enveloping the field.

I have no idea what the painting means. My incomprehension turns into irritation. I hate what I cannot fathom.

The waiter emerges from the steaming depths of the kitchen bearing a tray. I return to My dwelling place.

The waiter places the tray on the table.

On the tray is a wide plate of shells, an awl-shaped shucking knife, and a glass of frothy white foam.

The waiter says to My strong forearms, "Here's your oysters, Mister Frou-Frou."

"Here *are* your oysters," I correct him. "O never mind!"

He places My egg cream firmly on the table. The fermented fluid froths over.

Ignoring him, I suck the guts out of an oyster shell.

"I wish I was that oyster right now, Mister Pooh-Bah."

I say without looking at him, "Why? So that I could defecate you?"

He laughs mirthlessly, "Ha ha ... Ha."

I seize another oyster. My fingers prod the lid.

The waiter says slyly to My perfectly fashioned jaw, "Oysters's such sexy food."

I must get rid of him.

I ask the waiter pointedly, "Does this look 'sexy' to you?"

I thrust the shucking knife into the shell.

The slowly penetrating blade pierces the connecting muscle. I pry open the oyster, unhinging it with force.

Ohne Gewalt bekomme Ich Meine Austern nicht!

The crustacean exhales a profound sigh, its shell agape.

I point at the oyster's insides with the tip of the shucking knife.

Its tendons glimmer darkly.

A glistening, semiliquid secretion swirls over the supple fleshmeat.

I reach into the shell and pull out the moist, kneadable gut.

The attaching membranes tear. The waiter's teeth clack and clatter. He has never seen an oyster disemboweled before. His mouth widens. His cheeks flex.

His larynx is as black as a witch's gullet.

He screams and flees.

Watch out.

A desire surges within the sea of My mind, a kind of bubbly irritation.

It is time to harvest the fruits that grow in My erotic garden.

My penis is a scythe.

Perhaps I could have a quickie in the lavatory.

Dropping the oyster shell, I snatch a few tubs of whipped margarine and ascend from the table.

I rush to the back of the diner.

With urgency in My voice, I ask an aging dinerslut perched on a stool, "Do you have a mirror that I could use for a moment?"

The floozy hands Me her pocket mirror unquestioningly, her eyes dazed with longing.

Without thanking or acknowledging her, I whisk the pocket mirror from her waiting hands and run into the dank lavatory.

Locked in an untenanted stall, I study My reflection in the grease-smeared speculum.

Hot fuck, I am hot.

No one looks more dashing than Me.

Breathing vehemently, I open a tub of margarine and lather My penis with the creamy substance. An erection quickly begins to crystallize. I stroke My penis vigorously.

Someone has written on the door of the stall with an orange magic marker, "I WANT YOU."

I stroke My rapidly solidifying penis, lubricating it gently with the margarine. To intensify My pleasure, I lather My anus with the frothy goo. I girth My penis and cup its cap.

I am so beautiful that it breaks My heart.

I knead My testes, fondling them fondly. My penis is deliciously irritated. I delicately manipulate My perineum. A vigorous stream of thick, diaphanous fluid gushes out of My glans and splatters onto the door of the stall.

My penis detumesces.

Pearls of semen drip from its aperture. I wipe the slimy opalescence from My stomach with a paper towel.

I leave behind traces of gelatin wherever I go.

Sated, I slide slipperily out of the lavatory.

I hand the pocket mirror to the aging dinerslut without looking at her face.

I drift to My booth and swallow a wad of oyster intestines while staring languidly at My image in the window. My face is ghostly.

When I indulge in these moments of digestion, I am reminded that human beings are also food to be digested. They exist to be consumed, used up.

Wo die Welt Mir in den Weg kommt, da verzehre ich sie, um Meine allverzehrende Lust nach Herrschaft zu stillen.

I devour human beings — not literally, of course. I use them — and, in that sense, I "eat" them.

You strange creatures, you are nothing more to Me than a meal at the fast-food restaurant of life.

I eat from the lunch box of self-enjoyment.

You are nothing more to Me than a thing to be devoured; I will shovel down each one of you.

When I order food from the lobotomized waiter, I am using him; i.e., I am grinding him up with My teeth.

When I borrow a pocket mirror from the aging dinerslut, I am masticating her.

When I pay the desk clerk for a night at the Crystalline Hotel, I am swallowing him.

When Miss Grimmlager takes down My information, I am ingesting her.

They, the mob, are My nourishment.

Human beings are biodegradable.

The Decapitated Bull

I ooze out of Ye Olde Diner. Someone behind Me says in a loud voice:

"I WANNA TAKE MY GIRL TO THE MOTHERFUCKIN ZOO AND SHIT."

Look at the skyline, Jonathan Barrows. It is beautifully stained with popcorn butter.

Something that resembles an iridescent spacecraft glides across the deepening evening.

I stroll into the Decapitated Bull, a local Drink-and-Vomit on Impression Avenue. Peanut shells crackle under My feet. As I enter, the patrons stop talking.

Ils Me méprisent parce que ils M'aiment.

I look to My right. A woman with nauseatingly large breasts sits at a table surrounded by breast-hungry men. Yee-hah. She speaks girlspeak and is as attractive as microwaved roadkill.

"Richard gere likes gerbils but only when theyre declawd."

She notices Me, of course, like everyone does. It is to be expected that gazes will be drawn to Me.

I am the absolute self.
Everywhere I go, men and women follow Me with lascivious eyes.
My existence prompts them to commit bold acts.

The woman with nauseatingly large breasts approaches My table and sits down next to Me uninvited.

She is too close. Her movements are too brisk, too sudden, too feminine.

Joseph Suglia

The gaggle of men giggle. Their giggling is forced.

The woman's mouth deepens into a chasm. She says to My finely chiseled features, "Hi my names gina but you can call me gin for short everyone else does i love drinkin that gin do you mind if i sit here with you."

"I have come here for one purpose. I want a drink of absinthe, and then I'll be on My way. Time presses. Are you the waitress?"

"No im just one of the girls!"

I have no idea what that means, and neither does she.

She asks Me the same question that people always ask, "Whats your name?"

I look at the wall behind her and say with indifference, "You are in no position to address Me, Gabriela. There is no symmetry between us. My consciousness is entirely different from your own. However, if you were someone who was worthy of addressing Me, I would say, 'My name is Jonathan Barrows.'"

My intransitive, vacant gaze strikes her.

She says slowly, "I dont mean to disturb you but you just seem so peaceful."

Her mouth widens abyssally and out of the throbbing abyss issue words.

She speaks. As she speaks, her udders tremble.

The trembling of her udders unsettles Me.

"Did you see that busboy he really likes me i mean men just throw themselves at me and you can see why i can tell that you like me too just like all guys like that busboy who works here dont tell anyone but i gave him my number that was so chickeny of me sometimes i think like i dont have any balls i just break down and give guys my number even though i

know that i shouldnt i guess that im just a nice person at heart or maybe im just a big chicken he calls me like im not kidding he that bus boy i mean he has been calling me like once every day for the past month i mean ive been deleting all of his messages but just like last night i actually listened to one of his messages you know just for kicks and he started saying things like please gina just call me just once so like i did but that was just to like tell him to stop calling me i mean come on what does he think does he really think that i would like actually go out with him or have any respect for him at all after hes been like calling me for one full month straight i mean come on thats just ridiculous anyway i said on the phone that he was really nice and everything but that he just wasnt my type because im looking for a younger man and he is like thirty-nine which is way out of my ballpark i like guys between around thirty to thirty-three thats my age range but i mean in a few years he could be my father or something also hes a busboy this is like what his second job or something i want a guy with a good career and stuff not like some poor busboy who has to dig for change when he takes me to burger god although i mean like i really like burger dog i mean burger god ha ha ha and everything especially their chicken-powdered french fries they are like soooooo good you cant even believe it have you ever had the chicken-powdered french fries at burger god like they are like soooooo good i mean i can tell that you are a well-heeled guy you dress real nice and stuff and you look a lot like jude law and stuff anyway like that busboy he doesnt like know how to dress or anything like i mean im not talking about the way that he is dressing now you know like hes at work and everything but like i was like at ye olde diner and he

was off from work with his brother whos also kinda dorky and spanish like him they both look just like big insects or something and he that busboy i mean he was wearing i am not kidding you now he was like wearing stone-washed black jeans you know the speckly kind they had like white dots and stuff and ohmygod like i am not kidding he was even wearing like ohmygod i am not kidding he was wearing sneakers white sneakers ohmygod like that is like so nineties but then theres this other guy i know who works at the crystalline hotel as a day manager and stuff and hes really kinda cute and well built and my weakness is for like big arm muscles and stuff and he like had those all right and so anyway i was the one who approached him but i kinda knew right from the beginning like that the feeling was mutual especially when he complimented me on my chest as you noticed ive got like really big breasts fortyfour double ds and men like those a lot they get me into clubs for free and i dont even need to pay for meals anymore like but i am so a good girl i am not even kidding i am so serious i am very religious because my parents are religious are you religious too."

She speaks for My benefit. If I were not present to listen to her speak, she would have no reason to speak.

Speech requires a listener in order to exist as speech.

The singer is not a singer unless there are ears to hear her song.

The bird that sings does not sing alone.

I want to get rid of this she-creature. Very quickly. I will scandalize her; then she'll leave Me alone.

I say without looking at her, "I am a Christian, but I don't believe that a god exists beyond this world."

Befuddled, she stares at My immaculately fashioned face and asks, "Why why is that?"

"Because I AM God."

"What what do you mean what do you mean jesus is god."

The strobe light in her mind is fizzling out.

"Jesus of Nazareth was nothing more than a random lunatic who claimed to be God. That impostor. He could not have predicted My advent. I am the only God you'll ever need."

I hate all living things equally.
— Jonathan Barrows

Gabriela doesn't understand Me. Gabriela will never understand Me. Gabriela is not capable of understanding Me.

My interest in this idiotic woman is very low. Whenever she opens her mouth to speak, My interest in her weakens even more.

The train in her mind shunts tracks.

Gabriela says direly, "You know the rock that wrestler the rock i dated the rock."

I look around her pitilessly and say, "I wouldn't brag about that if I were you."

In a renewed attempt to gather My attention, Gabriela smirks and says slyly, "By the way i dye my anal hair red white and blue the colors of this great country of ours and stuff sometimes like on the fourth of july and stuff i bend down along the highway and spread open my ass cheeks so that the drivers and walkers can like see my dyed anal hair and stuff they

Joseph Suglia

usually the drivers in the cars they like usually honk their horns and cheer at me and stuff."

It is her patriotism, not her indiscreet remark, that troubles Me.

The strobe light in her mind reignites and then dims again.

She says to My grooved brow, "Ill tell you what mister lardy-dardy im looking for new candidates i have three boyfriends but you smell nice and dress nice and i think that you'd be a nice new candidate."

She does not want a new candidate. She wants Me to inject My juices into her body. She wants Me to infuse her life with meaning.

I must extricate Myself from the snare of this female bear trap.

I sigh and say without looking at her, "I'll only be here for a few days. I'm here for an interview at the community college. I don't have time for a relationship."

She asks My seraphic face, "Well what about a short-term relationship."

I look at her without pity and say, "A short-term relationship is too long for Me."

Gabriela is visibly shocked. No man has ever rejected her before.

She looks at Me as if a thick green tentacle were growing out of My ear.

I hoist Myself out of the chair. Open-mouthed and bewildered, she grips the sleeve of My tweed jacket.

Raising Myself, I detach her slime-slicked claw from My sleeve with force and jaunt toward the exit.

Watch out.

The breast-obsessed men glower at Me with spiteful envy.

For five years, they have haunted the Decapitated Bull with the intent of owning her desire. They roofed her with compliments and gestures. She captured their attention with vague promises of breast-flesh and spasm. I seized the desire of their beloved without even trying or wanting to. In a small town such as Benton Harbor, women like Gabriela are coronated. I have stolen their queen.

I am a refugee from the country of her desire.

As I hoof out of the Decapitated Bull, Gabriela locks her parasite eyes onto My buttocks. There is no question about it. My body is mega-protrusive.

She fixes her eyes and snarls.

She calls My name, an unheeded exhortation, and grasps at the air with adhesive hands.

Watch out.

I slide out of the Decapitated Bull and dash down the arterial streets, My lungs full of self-satisfaction.

Meeting the Neighbors

Exhausted by My adventures in the Decapitated Bull, I insinuate into the Crystalline Hotel without greeting the porter, who stares at Me inquiringly while pretending to read a multi-wrinkled issue of *Cosmopolitan* magazine.

I slither through the corridors like a well-lubricated colonoscope until I reach My hotel room.

I enter.

I stand transfixed before the mirror that hovers above the dresser.

Fixing My eyes upon My own image, I perform a slow and seductive striptease for Myself. I watch Myself gradually unraveling in the mirror. I am entranced by My performance.

I say to My own image, "Come on, whore! Strip, you fucking man-slut! Take it off, bitch! Show Me your penis, slut! Show it to Me, bitch! Come on, bitch! I want to see your testicles. Show Me your bouncing testicles, whore!

"SHOW ME THAT ASS! SHOW ME THAT ASS! COME ON, SLUT, SHOW IT TO ME!"

Hubba hubba hubba hubba hubba hubba hubba hubba hubba hubba hubba hubba hubba hubba hubba hubba hubba hubba hubba hubba!

Now I am delightfully undressed. The bed is littered with My deliciously embroidered undergarments.

Hot damn, I am hot.

What is this?

On My bed is a solitary white hair. Doesn't belong to Me. Did the former tenant leave this behind?

I need to distract My mind.

I turn on My television set and watch a popular situation comedy called *Becker*, previously known as *Hey, Becker!*, which stars Ted Danson as Doctor John Becker and Terry Farrell as Reggie. I think that I've seen this one before.

I dart My right index finger into My anus.
I am the most beautiful odalisque in My harem.

In this episode, Dr. Becker goes on a cruise. Unbeknownst to him, "The Pleasure Cruise" is, in fact, a gay cruise. There's "cruising" in more ways than one on that ship! Hilarity ensues when gay "cruisers" hit on Dr. Becker left and right. There's also a funny scene involving an effete cruise director, who I think is played by David Bowie, but I'm not exactly sure.

I silence the volume.

Dr. John Becker waves his hands at Me through the speculum of the cathode ray tube, smiling laughlessly. He seethes angrily through his teeth, his equanimity slowly slipping away. Goodbye, sanity. Goodbye.

Behind his joyless smile, he seems to say to Me, "HELP ME, JONATHAN BARROWS! PLEASE, FOR GOD'S SAKE, HELP ME!"

I turn on My portable cassette player and listen to My sonorous voice resonantly reading an essay by Saint Max.

I loop the tendrils of My testicular hair around My nimble fingers. Listening to the sound of My voice gets Me really hot. I tickle My glans and passionately massage My testicles. My fingertips dance playfully around My anal orifice. I slip them into its warm oven.

My penis quickly calcifies.

Stroke. Stroke. Stroke.

Fuck Me. Fuck Me.

It doesn't take long for Me to reach orgasm. A fine white mist squirts out of My penis.

I'd like a post-masturbatory cocktail. My libation of choice is lime-flavored seltzer water. There's a vending machine on this floor. I think that it has what I need.

I swathe My form in a semen-stained bathrobe and sinuate through the zigzagging corridors.

Bathrobed men and entoweled women stroll out of their night-chambers. The parade of dreamers has begun. I see the nightpeople strolling dispassionately through the hallways, led on by an unseen beacon.

It is time to meet the neighbors.

The ungiggling residents of the Crystalline Hotel gape at Me as I drift past them.

A mustached woman somnambulates out of her room, staring at Me with dead eyes.

Watch out.

The children of the residents clamber from their bedsheets, ready to scamper to the lower levels of the hotel. They watch Me intensely as I walk down these corridors of love.

Wherever I go, men and women follow Me with eyes of desire.

I reach the vending machine. I stick the money into its mouth. The machine rattles noisily; a bottle of lime-

flavored seltzer water spurts out. Within the bottle, a geyser is fomenting.

Clutching her bathrobe, the hairy woman asks, looking at Me through the crevices of her eyes, "Who are you, Mister Smarty Pants?"

I respond unhesitatingly, "I am your master, cunt."

Nasal hair sprouts from her nostrils.

I stride down the corridor toward My hotel room with supreme self-assurance. Walking with seltzer in hand, I notice a pack of unmoored women drifting ahead of Me.

I feel strangely abstracted from this spiral of events. Watching from the harbor of an alcove, I wait for the noctambulating women to disappear into the shelter of their hovels.

Someone — I think it was the great nineteenth-century French novelist Joris-Karl Huysmans — once said, "People who are in pain do loathsome things."

The hotel-dwellers feel their own unimportance in relation to My greatness and, for this reason, suffer the most atrocious agonies imaginable.

Because they are in pain, they are capable of committing the most salacious acts of vengeance.

Once they discover that I am a genius, they grow resentful of My brilliance.

Filthy animals, they seek out ways of punishing Me for My greatness. Hollow-headed creatures, they despise Me in order not to despise themselves.

Vous Me méprisez pour ne pas vous mépriser.

Each one of them is deeply preoccupied with Me. Every woman wants Me. Every man wants to be Me.

For I am like a swan levitating above the fetid swamp that is the Crystalline Hotel.

Crystalline water flows over My feathers.

The fungus of the swamp does not adhere to My immaculate plumage.

Vandalism

Wednesday pops up like a jack-in-the-box.
The common people walk to their vehicles and drive
to work with heavy eyes. They punch their time cards.
They cannot stop the incessant clanging that
sounds in their ears.
Wearing nothing other than a snug pair of J.B.
swimming trunks, I sun Myself on the grassy plain
behind the Crystalline Hotel.
I am lying prostrate on My Zarathustra beach
blanket. Globules of sunlight rain on My forehead.
Some of the residents gaze at Me from the seclusion
of their balconies. To taunt them, I fold up My
swimming trunks so that they resemble a thong. Most
of My buttocks are revealed.
A vixenish girl with cropped black hair scrutinizes
Me, leaning upon a balustrade.
YOU WANT IT, BUT YOU CAN'T HAVE IT, BITCH!
Other residents are stirred by the sight of My hilly
buttocks, as well.
Through the palisades, I see a shame-eyed middle-
aged man sipping a brimming cup of licorice tea while
staring at the tufts of My anal hair.
I'M TURNING YOU ON, AM I NOT?
I knead a part of My body that I love particularly,
the nape of My neck as it bleeds into My shoulder
blade.
My chest is radiant. I slather My bulbous biceps
with tanning foam until they glisten.
On My Walkman is the essay, "*Das unwahre Prinzip
unserer Erziehung oder Humanismus und Realismus,*"
composed by Saint Max and read by Present
Company.
Hot damn. It is time to masturbate.

In a languorous swoon, I drift into the Crystalline Hotel.

The desk clerk pants as I shimmy into the lobby. He studies My buttocks, which are conspicuously visible through My swimming trunks.

I look down and notice that My penis is standing upright. What could be more lovely than the tumefaction of My penis?

I take the elevator to the third floor and ambulate into My hotel room.

I unclose the door and float inside.

My window is agape like the mouth of a cloudy sperm whale.

A sheen of light shimmers on the fuzzed carpet.

Watch out.

A winnowing wind billows through My window.

My papers rustle conspicuously underneath My desk.

My inflatable love doll lies sodden, deflated on the carpet.

A cloud of human rot hangs heavily in the air.

My penis photographs, curled up and disused, are disseminated throughout My room.

A videotape of My penis, unshelled of its cartridge, lies untended on My desk. My suitcase balloons open.

I cast My eyes back and forth.

On the wall over My bed are spray-painted the words, "YOU AINT THE CENTER OF THE FUCKIN WORLD."

The words, frank and stark, are orange, a color that I despise. Orange is the most vulgar color; it is redolent of the mob.

I ask no one in particular, "Who has eaten My porridge?"

The garbage can has been toppled over. My trash is strewn lazily on the floor.

I saunter to My lavatory.

A putrid brown banana breathes heavily on the tiles like a de-aquariumed fish.

The walls are splattered with a thick sheen of Mango-Kiwi Awareness Shampoo.

A viscous puddle of ooze spreads across the slick porcelain floor.

Passion Fruit Explosion Hand Lotion drips down the shower curtain in messy dollops.

My electric razor lies unhooked and neglected in My sink.

Enraged, I pick up My telephone and dial the front desk. The hotel clerk answers.

"Crystalline Hotel. How may I serve you?"

"This is Jonathan Barrows."

There is no response.

"Someone vandalized My hotel room."

At first, there is silence.

"Like, what did they, like, do?"

"They opened My suitcase and cast all of My possessions around the room ... They upset the garbage can and emptied My shampoo bottle. They even spray-painted a message on the wall."

"How do you, like, know it was a 'they'? Who did the vandalizing?"

"I don't know. Someone."

"So you think it was just one person who trashed your room? What if it was a gang?"

"I don't know how many people were involved."

"You don't know, like, how many people were involved?"

"No, I don't know."

"Well what if it was ... like, an animal or something?"

"I don't care *who* or *what* strewed My things around. I just want My room cleaned up."

"Was anything stolen? Why don't you, like, call the police?"

"The police are not professional cleaners. And nothing was stolen, as far as I can see. I am not going to telephone the police. They are probably just as incompetent as everyone else in Benton Harbor ... Listen, this simply isn't *the issue*. I want My hotel room cleaned up. Now!"

The desk clerk pauses and sighs with audible frustration.

"Well, what do you want me to do about it?"

"Let Me repeat for the purposes of emphasis: *I want you to come and clean up My hotel room.*"

"That ain't my job."

The desk clerk is silent for a moment.

"That ain't my job at all."

"Get someone else to do it, then!"

"Like, who?"

"Why not the maid?"

"The maid?"

"Yes, the maid! Get the maid to come and clean up My fucking hotel room!"

"The maid's off today."

"What?"

"I said, 'The maid's off today.'"

"What the hell does that mean?"

"She went home. She's, like, really tired and shit."

"Am I correct in assuming that there is only one maid in this wretched hotel?"

"No, sometimes I'm, like, the maid. But a male maid and shit. I mean, I sometimes just do the shit that she does, when she's not, like, working and shit. But I'm not really the maid or anything."

"Then why don't *you* clean up My fucking hotel room?"

"I'm busy. I've got to ... I've got to watch the desk and check people in and clean up the lobby and shit."

"Who is going to clean up *My hotel room?*"

The desk clerk keeps silence for a moment. He asks My ear, "Why don't you clean it up?"

"Why don't I clean it up? Because that's what you helots are paid to do!"

"What's that mean?"

"What does *what* mean?"

"'Hellet.'"

"*Helot.* I said, 'helot'! A 'helot' is a slave — a slave like you!"

"I ain't your slave. The maid ain't your slave, either. She's not, like, your personal cleaner or anything. She ain't your whore."

"Listen, I want this taken care of. If you are not capable of cleaning My hotel room or following simple instructions — and evidently this is the case — I want someone else to clean it, and I want it done now."

"There's nothing I can do, Mister Hoity-Toity."

He hangs up.

Because I sexually rejected him, he despises Me. Because he despises Me, he will not accommodate My demands.

I promenade to My lavatory.

My toothpaste is mysteriously intact.

I brush My teeth vehemently, rubbing the firm razor blade bristles against My ruby gums.

My teeth feel foamy fresh.

I throw Myself on My bed, rip off My clothing, and passionately caress My beautiful nipples.

Watch out.

Something viscid sticks to My hands. Thick ultraslime moistens My palms. The intruder left a sprawling trail of fermented liquid on the sheets.
I lift Myself and amble toward My window.
I stare at the landscape.
The landscape is not dead.

Walter the Pig

I'm in the lobby of the Crystalline Hotel reading My translation, *The Unique Individual and Its Property.* Every now and then, I stealthily massage the tip of My penis with My free hand.

I want Myself. I want Myself badly.

I want to manipulate My perineus muscle. I want to massage My testicles. I want to slather My penis with margarine. I want to fuck Myself savagely. I want to insert My penis into My doll's colostomized anus.

The desk clerk reads Me as I read. He envies My unrippled placidity.

I have timeless time to devote Myself to the joys of the intellect. He does not.

An American tourist of the most typical variety meanders through the lobby, humming to himself unmelodically. He passes Me, halts, then reverses.

He ejaculates into My ear, "That looks like an interesting book!"

I say nothing.

He asks, "Whatcha readin'?"

I respond, "Strings of letters."

Letters couple and uncouple, filaments of words.

He pauses and then asks, "If you could sum up the whole book in one sentence, what would it be?"

"I could summarize the entire text in three words."

He guffaws defiantly and blurts out, "Really? What words would those be?"

"LEAVE ME ALONE!"

I raise Myself suddenly and ascend the staircase with a buoyant gait. The tourist is invisible, reduced to oblivion.

Joseph Suglia

*The worst thing that one can do to the other person is
ignore him.*

Or amputate his arms.

— Jonathan Barrows

I weave into My hotel room and see an old man
spread-eagled on My wrinkled bedsheets. His face
slackened and miserable, the old man tumbles and
turns restively.

Out of his mouth cascade unsolid globs of yogurt.

His eyelids are peeled back, revealing fresh white
orbs. He growls and scowls bestially. He would look
like David Bowie, if David Bowie were frozen in a meat
locker for a year.

Watch out.

Like a burnt-out geriatrician whose contempt for his
patients is only slightly veiled, I approach the old man
and shout, "Get up, and get the fuck out!"

Fucking Geritol® addict.

The old man squirms. As he shifts his body, I recoil
in raw horror.

He is wearing a yellow pair of boxer shorts. Through
the boxer shorts bulges a wizened scrotum-sac.

His unshaven countenance mangled in distortions
of pain, the old man glowers.

His hands involuntarily grope and scratch the
plasma-stained bedsheets in a pantomime of human
agony.

He balls into a serpentine mass and unmellowly
moos.

His awkward, unconsciously winking right eye
waters at its wrinkled terminus.

58

Tossing his age-whitened head on the sleep-drenched pillow, he widens his maw like a disemboweled lion.

He is like an animal that has been trained to imitate the mannerisms of human beings.

The pillow deflates.

In a hollow daze, I ask him, "Excuse Me, what are you doing in My hotel room?"

No response.

"How did you get in?"

He cries, "*Wa wa wa wa wa wa wa wa wa!*"

I don't care why he is here.

I just want the old fucker to leave.

Should I telephone hotel security? That would only gather unwanted attention. I will inveigle him out of My hotel room instead. How to do this? I will feign compassion.

Feigned sympathy may be an effective way of achieving your goals.
— Jonathan Barrows

Like a disaffected morgue attendant, I crouch down beside the bed and ask the old man super-softly, "Tell Me ... Tell Me, what ails you, My elderly friend? Why are you in My hotel room? How may I offer you ... My assistance?"

The old man springs to life.

He exclaims, "Well, Mister Namby-Pamby, this isn't exactly *your* hotel room, you know. I lived in this room for thirty years before you moved in. That's probably as long as you've been alive, young man. Me and my sister, Winnie, we lived here together."

He is lying. They could not have possibly afforded to live here for thirty years. The Crystalline Hotel is a cheap lodging, but it's not cheap enough for his kind.

Mendacious old fool. Bilious slob.

"You young people treat your elders with the greatest irreverence because you are afraid of growing old yourselves. But we must all walk down that long path that leads to the great unknown and ..."

I do not want to listen to this.

"I was young once, too. Do not forget that, young man. When I was your age, I lived here with Winnie. I hardly ever lurked outside of the Crystalline. Winnie kept me harnessed to this bed. Sometimes, she tied me up in a hammock and suspended me in the air. She fed me liquid oatmeal."

With an affected tone of sympathy, I say, "That must have been dreadful for you."

"In confidence, young sir, I will tell you that I hadn't the slightest care one way or the other! Had she not bound me with fetters, I would have suggested the punishment myself!"

The strung harness tightened as he struggled; the ceaseless tugging of his arms firmed the bonds.

Unsure of why I am participating in this seemingly pointless conversation, I ask, "Why, exactly, did your sister tie you to the bed?"

Limp coupons excised from a coupon book litter My bed, curled cheeseparings. I pick up one of the coupons and hold it in front of My face.

The old man sputters, "I see you looking at my coupons. Yes, I've got coupons for Lobster King! Do you want one? Well, that's too bad! They're mine! All mine!"

Playing the role of the concerned physician, I repeat my question, "Why did your sister, as you say, harness you to the bed?"

With a melancholy air, the old man stares at the cracked egg-shell ceiling and says, "It had to be the way that it had to be. Winnie was afraid that I'd hurt myself. I went a little crazy, you understand, because I lost the girl of my dreams. For the thirty years that I lived in this room, I mourned her. Her name ... was Margarita."

Dear God or whomever, I do not want to listen to this.

As he speaks, the furrows on his face unsuture, spreading open.

"I met Margarita at the Burger God in St. Joseph, where she worked. Ever since I first set eyes on her, I imagined the joy that she and I would someday share. We would lounge on the beaches. The sea slugs would dance only for us. The gulls would dive down from the sky and retrieve the fish innards scattered on the sandy ground. I would crouch over the slickenside of a searock and write a poem in honor of that which she would inspire in me — the limitless enchantment of love. There was a long line of patrons at that Burger God, but I would not be deterred. I ran in front of the queue, leapt over the counter, and began to kiss her softly on the cheeks, lips, forehead, and anus. She drew back. Cruel woman! 'Help meeeeeeeeeee!' she cried and screamed for the manager, pulling my hands from her tender young dugs. Those words scarified my soul.

"I was inconsolable. I mourned her something fierce, my darling inamorata Margarita. She is the reason that I am the way that I am today. My dear darling sister Winnie had to make sure that I wouldn't do

myself any harm. She even bought me a pig to console me. To help me get over my blessed girl Margarita. The pig's name was Walter. Like me. My name's Walter, too."

Exhausted, I sit down in My chair. I shield My eyes with My hands, sighing plaintively.

"Walter lived with us for only a week. A week until the Crystalline management found out about him living here, living here with me. One of the neighbors must've complained. The people here at the Crystalline, they're so malicious. We had to find Walter a new home or else face eviction. A farm in St. Joseph accepted our dear Walter. He lived there for a year. I visited him every day of that pig's blessed life. The old farmer, Jacob was his name, was so kind to us. He even gave Walter his own private shelter, his own little pen.

"Then, one day, something terrible happened ..."

A coy cat slithered through the interstices of the fence that bordered the pen. Walter lurked in the silent mud. He was motionless, but his eyes followed the cat as it sinuated into his domain.

The cat playfully sauntered through the sludge and played with a dandelion that drifted on the surface of a mud puddle.

Walter's eyes began to vibrate.

Suddenly, Walter threw his body forward and plunged his teeth into the cat's hide. He grasped the cat in his mouth and thrashed his head back and forth vehemently. Damp clumps of black fur flew in all directions.

Walter dropped the cat, now reduced to a matted carpet, into a mud puddle. Mud splashed onto Walter's thick hide.

The cat, still alive, crept softly out of the mud puddle.
His eyes glowing with rage, Walter lunged again and
seized the cat in his mouth.

"After the incident, Farmer Jacob had to quarantine Walter. There was nothing else to be done. Farmer Jacob locked Walter in the barn ..."

His lachrymose eyes threaten to eject granules of tears.

"That was where he'd see his final days. The barn rats. They fell on him. The next morning there wasn't even a carcass. Only a skeleton with all of the meat, organs, and skin chewed away."

Walter was a pig. He lived on a farm in St. Joseph.
Walter the pig, you are gone.
Walter the pig, you are no more.
Walter the pig, you were devoured by the barn rats.

Staring into My eyes to gauge My level of sympathy, the old man shifts his position on the bed.

He protrudes his tongue as if he wanted to lick My eyebrows, gropes his withered scrotum, and plays with the white pubic hairs that line his smegma-stained testicles.

I have lost all patience. I want the senile fool gone. Now.

Suddenly anxious, I ask the old man, "You have a key, don't you? Will you return the key?"

He does not respond.

I scream at the old man imperatively, "GET OUT OF MY HOTEL ROOM NOW, YOU FILTHY GRANDMOTHERFUCKER!"

My voice ringing with hatred, I ask him again, "Do you have A KEY? DO YOU?"

Without answering, the old man dunks his head into the watery bedsheets and rolls around in the waves. He strains his flabby, muscleless arms upward.

I rummage through My suitcase. I will drive the old man out with My hairbrush.

I see the old man's mouth open and close.

His mouth lusts for raw meat — rubicund, pungent, plump hunks of cowfruit.

A Knock on the Door

I am in My bedclothes daydreaming.

I dream of Me dancing down a streamside lane, My penis flopping up and down gracelessly in the wind.

The object of sexual desire is never elegant.

Heterosexual men find breasts stimulating for the same reason that heterosexual women find penises stimulating. Because they look absurd. Breasts and penises are grotesque and for that reason are stimulating.

An orgasm is a response to an irritation.
Irritation causes fluid to flow from the body.
What irritates the body is the grotesque.
— Jonathan Barrows

The bed sinks Me into itself, a fortress comfortably massaging My sides like a lover.

A penumbra softens My vision.

I drove the old man out with My hairbrush. I struck his head over and over again, cattle-prodding him with the brush until he departed voluntarily. After the old fool had been evacuated, I bolted into the lobby and acquired a fresh set of bedsheets from the desk clerk.

I must pay My hotel bill before noon. I'll stay here for another day.

The sun streams pleasantly through the window. Beautiful sunlight cream, fluent pudding.

I turn on My television set, smiling with self-complacency, and watch a few minutes of the hit sitcom, *Becker*.

In this episode, Margaret (Hattie Winston) has a sexual dream about Dr. Becker. Her head full of lust, she tosses in her bed, grasping her breasts. Her eyes

sheen with enraged desire. She quivers like a rutting squirrel. Salvia-frost spews from her mouth in spurts as she undergoes paroxysms of desire.

Watch out.

Some worthless buffoon is knocking on the door.
What is this? Go away.
I shamble toward the door through curtains of sunlight.
I twist the knob. A woman wearing a cellophane raincoat appears before Me.
Here is the translucent woman. Around her head whirls a happy nimbus. Her kangaroo eyes flicker.
I remember her vaguely. Where have I seen her before? Was it in the lobby? She must be a neighbor.
The stranger stands there and waits. She has the leer of the slave on her mouth.
A fluttering of wet lips masks an obsequious grin.
The woman tousles her overgrown bullion hair and asks Me, "Do you wanna see my thong?"
I rub My eyes. Is this happening?
"What?"
"I said, 'Do you wanna see my thong?'"
"What ... What are you saying to Me, she-thing?"
"My name's Mandy, Mister Nimble Toes. Here, let me show you my thong."

Watch out.

The stranger unbuckles the pink belt that lassoes her mayonnaise-stained jeans. She pulls down her jeans ostentatiously and displays to Me her zebra-striped thong-backed underwear. Like most women,

she adamantly refuses to accept the inexorable progress of aging.

As she lowers her body, I shrink back in disgust. One can see her veined breastly protuberances, obscenely askew, jutting out of her shirt.

Outside of My window, clouds break apart into strands of fissile tissue.

Hideous. Now she. Now she is turning around. No, no: not. Her anus is a creased vat of skin.

Yee-hah.

The nape of My neck shivers in still frisson. Horrified, I recoil.

"Thongs are really attractive, don't you think?"

"Only on horses. Listen, Miss Roly-Poly, would you kindly leave Me alone?"

Through the stranger's mouth issue indecipherable gymnastics of speech.

Gurgling and groaning, she sidles against the wall and squirms past Me. She caught Me off My guard, and now she is inside of My hotel room. I will do anything — absolutely anything — to drive her out of My private living space.

She has the aura of the charnel house about her.

Her eyes could rape you dry.

A clownish grimace mapping her mouth, the stranger says, "I am so hot that you could fry eggs on my bra."

Apparently, she believes what she says. Her protruding elbow hits My bedpost.

I say without looking at her, "Thank you for this delightful visit. Unfortunately, I am preoccupied ..."

She says/asks in a lisping drawl, "Whatsamatter don't you like girls?"

She turns around, scanning My hotel room. Her eyes shape its contours.

Thank God or whomever, her crevassed anus is concealed.

If I seem more aggressive, that will surely drive her out of My lair.

"Do you really consider yourself to be a 'girl'? You are an aging barslut."

"I'm thirty-five, Mister Nimble Toes. I've still got some good years ahead of me."

Use her name. Pretend to be sympathetic.

"Manuela, listen to Me. Let Me put this into a language that you could understand ..."

"My name's Mandy!"

"All right then, 'Mandy.' You are no more important to Me than a random coil of donkey faeces sprawled on the cobblestones of a suburban street."

"I'm sorry?"

Her mind is dissolving into a translucent pool of brain-sludge.

As I speak to this noisome woman, I inject thoughts into My penis, which grows to the extent that I reflect upon it.

"Manuela, perhaps the best way to make you understand would be to draw an analogy to a popular children's cartoon. Have you ever seen the film, *Pinocchio*?"

Emboldened, My penis stands proudly at attention, jutting conspicuously through My monogrammed trousers.

My erection has nothing to do with the vaginal creature that stands before Me.

Her arms akimbo on her waist, the intruder says with sarcasm and perceptible irritation:

"Yes!"

"Well, let's just say that I'm a bit like the character after which that film was named."

She glowers at Me defiantly and asks, "Why, are you, like, a wooden puppet?"

"No, Manuela. The matter is quite different." Staring through her as if she were made of Saran Wrap, I say archly, "I've got no strings. Got no strings to hold Me down."

Transparent, Manuela unsmiles winterly.

Watch out.

I wave My hands madly in a Cab Calloway impersonation and spin and pirouette around in a semicircle and then briskly shove the intruder out of My hotel room with both hands.

She collapses in the corridor, withering like a dead animal.

Her skin furrows and shrinks.

I close the door in her shock-contorted face.

Something must be done to erase the image of her many-fissured buttocks from My memory.

With an intense feeling of self-satisfaction, I return to My bed and try to ignore the insistent knocking that resonates through My darkened hotel room.

I think of My buttocks, their curved form. Desire crests in My gut. Breathless, I remove My bedclothes. I grip My penis and moan. I cradle My oyster-shaped testicles and sigh.

Semen is ever-secreting lifesap.
A geyser of semen is a volcanic inferno.

I feel such passion for Myself.

Noise

Sleep is impossible.

Is it Wednesday night or is it Thursday morning what time is it on the clock?

I'm sick and miserable and miserable and sick.

I paid the desk clerk his lump. I'll stay in this wretched hotel one more day. I'll find out what is going on tomorrow today tomorrow Thursday. Then I'll return home on Friday. I'll leave at full speed and never look back again.

I demand an interview.

I don't want to teach here anymore. These people are stupid and penurious. There's no amusement in it.

Nonethenever, I demand an interview.

My eyes are softened by the midnight ebony. I'm alone with the music of My mind. But what's this now?

A crackling cracking crashing comes from above My head. A steady dripping coming from the ceiling.

Toppling wind-worn pillars.

Noise. The neighbors are making noise.

Someone — I think it was the great German philosopher Arthur Schopenhauer — once wrote: "The mind is like a diamond."

Noise fractures that diamond, the darkly glimmering solitaire. With every blow of noise that strikes it, the diamond's value worsens.

Poets take precautions against the sunlight.
Philosophers take precautions against the intrusion of noise.
— Jonathan Barrows

Music blasts into My ears.

Cold cash, I've got the stash
Eatin' hash wit' the yellow mash

Columns of noise permeate the walls. They shamble toward Me now, slopping their way across the low-ceilinged hotel room.

Watch out.

They encircle the bed, jittering manically. All around Me now are squalling currents of noise.

Watch out.

A pall of noise shadows My head. It comes to rest on My oak-broad shoulders.
A thick cord of noise lingers in the air for a moment and then breaks apart.
The strand of noise sizzles as it dissolves. It foams into syrupy globs that splotch the bed.
Noise stretches across the ceiling, droops down, and nudges the lamp. The noise obtrudes.
The noise that reverberates through My hotel room is more corporeal than the bodies that produce it.

Watch out.

The noise is solid.
Above Me, a girlarm knocks a lamp to the floor. I feel as if that same object were striking My head.
Last night, a fist slammed My door. When the blow fell, I felt it resounding against My back.
A deafening cacophony of rap-rock hip-hop bling-blang adult alt or whatever it is that they call it these days ripples through the walls.

So pleased with all of your good wishes, all your dreams and all your hopes.
So pleased with all your sympathications, all your letters and all your notes ...
I should've known that we could never be friends. So why don't we bring this whole damn thing to an end?
YOU'RE NOT MY GIRLFRIEND!
YOU'RE NOT MY GIRLFRIEND!
YOU'RE NOT MY GIRLFRIEND!
LEAVE ME ALONE!
Stop leavin' notes under my door, girl.
I don' wanna see you 'round here no mo'.
Stop callin' me at work, bitch.
Get out of my life, ho, and off my porch ...
I should've known that we could never be friends.
So why don't we bring this whole damn thing to an end?
YOU'RE NOT MY GIRLFRIEND!
YOU'RE NOT MY GIRLFRIEND!
YOU'RE NOT MY GIRLFRIEND!
LEAVE ME ALONE!

The electronic drum machine blares. A noisy girl screams in joy.

I envisage her before Me. She resembles a wild pig or an angry boar. Her voice, porcine, squeezes obtrusively through the cracked wall.

I place *The Unique Individual and Its Property* face-down upon My pillow.

I raise and thrust Myself out of the room. I will find the noise-makers. The vociferatresses.

Generally speaking when people make noise they are intruding in your life-sphere they are encroaching upon your solitude infringing upon your private world

when they make noise they are where they do not belong there is no essential difference between someone who invades your hotel room and someone who loudens her voice and her movements she prevents Me from getting some good shut-eye a noise-maker transgresses your boundaries.

Loping through the corridors like a crazed horse, I reach the neighboring hotel room and rap loudly on the door.

A dark splatter, a bonerattling, a sledgehammering echoes in My mindspace.

The door bulges open lewdly.

Watch out.

Two rubber girls waver in front of Me youngly and slimily.

They introduce themselves.

"My name's Buttermilk."

"My name's Sasha."

"We're in a girlband kalled Girl Auction. We're driving to Detroit for a show and thought we'd stop here for a night."

I did not query them; this information comes un-requested.

"I dwell below you, and I would like the music silenced for the night."

Butterworth asks My shiny bulging pectoral muscles, "Who *in Sam's hell* do you think you are?"

I gambol into the hotel room, waving My hands wildly. My eyes are shining like the moon.

"Who am I? I am Jonathan Barrows, and I am infinitely more intelligent, infinitely more attractive, and infinitely more charming than you."

Sushi says slyly to Butterworth, "Not only is he kute as hell. He's also kinda stuck on himself. Playin hard to get."

Like all women, she is irreversibly drawn to Me in the way that maggots are drawn to sautéed duck in orange sauce.

Clouds of white frost move spectrally and languorously into the eye of the cathode ray tube.

Butterworth says to My super-gorgeous eyes, "You smell so nice Mister Super-duper that we kan forgive you for the mean things you say."

The way to a girl's heart is through her nasal passages.
— Jonathan Barrows

Sushi asks My firm buttocks, "How kan you not love this music?"

I reply, "This is not music. Music, in the true sense of the word, is the music of thought. This noise leads you away from yourself. It destroys concentration."

Bursting from the stereo system is an overloud David Bowie song entitled "I'm Ashamed of Americans" or something along those lines.

Typical *bimbot* rock, and yet the noise girds Me.

It imprisons Me in its firm coils.

Watch out.

The girls gyrate to the music, their stomachs inflating and hollowing madly.

Their bodies throb and spasm. Whiteness peers through their gabardine chemises.

I hear the silent roar of the woodland quails.

Joseph Suglia

They hoola-hoop with invisible hoola-hoops, their breasts shaking phrenetically like plastic bags laden with moist plaster. The noise resonates through the cavities of My cranium.

Watch out.

Butterworth grapples Sushi and fetters her flaccid arms while greedily fondling pockets of her adipose tissue. Her freed flesh flows generously.

The girls protrude their tongues simultaneously, interlocking them into a spreading, shimmering thread of chewing gum-empurpled skin. It seems as if the two solitary members are interwoven into one essence, a uniform tongue.

Yee-hah.

"Look, Daughters of the Succubus, none of this is turning Me on. If you really want to get Me excited, why don't you TURN THE FUCKING MUSIC DOWN and LEAVE ME THE FUCK ALONE?"

Sushi smiles at Me a servile smile and de-amplifies the volume.

"Anything you desire Mister Super-Duper."

She penetrates My generous chest with her eyes, moistens her lips with her tongue, and says ruttishly, "I love looking at male nipples. Show me your male nipples."

"I don't want to hear this," I say and dart elegantly toward the door, screening My paps with modest hands.

Sushi blocks My access.

"LET ME SEE YOUR MALE NIPPLES! I WANNA SEE YOUR MALE NIPPLES!"

"No!" I cry and back away.

Sushi lifts her antelope eyes knowingly and says, "You know you remind me of my kousin Joshua. You have the same eyebrows as him. When we were kids we used to play hopscotch and lick the worm off the pavement, which was fun on hot and sticky days. My kousin Joshua really liked me didn't he Buttermilk? I didn't think anything of it until I turned eighteen. Then he said hey babe let's go to Lobster King. I thought it was strange that my kousin would kall me babe. He took me out on a date to Lobster King. But I didn't like know that it was a date or anything. I love Lobster King ..."

A waiter strode out of the kitchen bearing a platter on which were precariously balanced a pitcher of water and plates of shrimp and scallops. The waiter had superhuman poise, it seemed, as he turned into the concourse.

The pitcher tipped and fell into the lobster tank, splashing polluted green water onto Joshua and Sushi.

Joshua's face was a mask of fear.

The waiter tripped, waving his arms in a Jerry Lewis impersonation, and fell head-first into the waiting lobster tank, bursting its foundations, causing an artificial waterfall, filled with groping monstrosities, to cascade onto the bordering tables.

The heaving platter catapulted through the air.

A platoon of spoons fell to the ground, parachutists without parachutes cartwheeling through space.

A bowl of lobster bisque flew up like a breaching whale, secreting its reddish-purple gunk into the broadening eyes of the red-haired waitress.

As the lobster tank shattered, shards of glass sprayed onto the hands of the patrons.

Joseph Suglia

Jets of water struck out in every direction. The repulsive aquatic beasts slithered out of the jagged remains of the tank and splattered noisily onto the restaurant floor.

The tiles were wet with bubbling plasma. Waiters and waitresses danced around in a frenzy, spluttering madly.

The collapsed waiter lay face-down in his lobster tank.

Fragments of broken glass poked into his chest, causing a steady stream of blood-syrup to spew from his wounds. Torrents of green flooded the restaurant, tendrils rolling across the tiled floor.

The deluge streamed into the kitchen.

A community of lobsters scrambled toward the exits.

They danced merrily on the grass-blades.

Springing up, the patrons leapt onto their tables.

An elderly couple dove behind the bar.

"After we left Lobster King, he said you owe me babe for the lobster. That's what kousin Joshua said. He drove us to the Burger God parking lot. Then he put on these white gloves you know the kind that surgeons wear and shit. Then he slobbered all over my neck and tried to hike up my skirt from behind and pull down my panties and stick his fingers into my asshole. I feeled the latex gloves all over my ass. I yelled stop it you fuckin pervert what the fuck do you think you're doin? He stank like a dead lobster that'd been left out in the air for too long. He shoved his hand under my skirt and started to play with my asshole, and then he licked my ears. He said give me some of that sweet lovin babe we arc relatives and so we should love one another. That's when I took off my shoe and started to

pound him with it. His face bleeded, and his nose got smashed.

"And then there was this time when I was in the big mall and I bent over to look at some perfume in the display kase. I kould tell that some old fuck was staring at my ass behind me kause we girls have a special sense for that kind of thing. Then the old fuck just kame over to me and started to kiss my face. He said give me a kiss my little lassie just kall me big uncle there's nothing wrong with a little human affection between a niece and her elder. And so I took off my shoe and beat him on the head with it until his ears started to leak these big globs of white pus. I'm so serious. Huge blobs of white shit started komin out of his ears. It was so gross. So many guys follow me around in the big mall and shit and try to grab my thighs or kiss me on the neck but if they do then they deserve what's komin to them."

Butterworth is perceptibly irritated, seemingly aware that tales of sexual molestation may be misimplemented as seduction strategies.

She attempts to pull My attention away from Sushi. She resembles an ox-driver pulling a bull over a wooden bridge. Her eyes batten themselves on My neck muscles.

She says, "You know, *Kavalier* once offered me $10,000 to pose in their *Book of Transparent Lingerie.*"

I say unblinkingly, "I would offer you twice that sum to keep your clothing on."

Sushi is still dazed by the traumas of her past — or, perhaps, stunned by My cutting repartee. She stares listlessly into silence.

A solemn, lightless space surrounds her.

She cannot free the apes that are locked in the cages of her mind.

Joseph Suglia

Butterworth rolls her eyeballs around twice and labializes with forced salaciousness, "You should be nicer to us if you want what you want. All three of us could have some fun together Mister Super-duper."

I ask disingenuously, "Doing what?"

"Doin some sexin."

They want to have a filthy orgy.

They want Me to irrigate their fields.

They want Me to fertilize their gardens.

They want Me to plow their fields.

They want Me to enrich their gardens.

They want Me to manure their plantation.

They want Me to harvest their plantation.

The threesome is the poetry of the mob.
— Jonathan Barrows

I say to them sharply, "I do not have sex. I do have *coitus interruptus*, however."

Sushi asks My magical eyes, "So you want to pull out before you nut?"

Butterworth affirms, "That kould work."

I shake My head and say, "No. I would rather interrupt sexual intercourse indefinitely."

My words are directed at no one in particular. Neither of the girls understands. I reach for the door.

Watch out.

Dazedly, Butterworth attempts to block My passage.

She spreads her latex claws. I slide smoothly and dazzlingly out of the room with the grace of a professional skater.

I say to Sushi's sunken, shrunken, disbelieving face as I pass, "You are the result of an unhappy abortion."

I saunter lazily down the corridor. I am so graceful and elegant. I stick a dollar into the mouth of the vending machine.

A bottle of lime-flavored seltzer water spurts out of the dispenser.

I choke the bottle 'til My knuckles whiten. I twist open the cap.

The mustached woman lolls in the corridor, watching Me charily with malicious eyes.

The liquid burgeons forth vehemently, bubbling with refreshing effervescence.

I return to My hotel room, glowing with sweet self-complacency.

Against the window spreads the mellifluous plasma of the vanishing daylight. Sun-slime drips down the pane.

The sun oozes smoothly into the room. Incandescent globules of light flow onto the carpet.

I ignite the television set and watch a few minutes of the popular sitcom, *Becker.* In this episode, the incessant flickering of a flashing street light prevents Dr. Becker from sleeping. Despite the fact that he consumes nearly everything on the pharmacological menu, his sleeplessness remains tragically unalleviated.

Suspended in the infinite night, he can neither live nor die.

His eyes are pried open against his conscious intentions. He cannot stem the flood of thoughts that infiltrate his brain.

After a week of insomniac nights, the doctor completely loses his sense of space-time.

His psychotic episode is historically unpleasant.

While turning in his bed, he screeches silently, his mouth widening and twitching spasmodically. He is absent to himself, an angry skull with blazing eyes.

I place My priapic member between the thumb and forefinger of My right hand. I stroke Myself into a froth. I throw Myself into ecstasy.

I am a semen explosion waiting to happen.

I leap onto My bed and squirm around in the sheets. Spent, My vision fading, I drift into somnolence.

My sleep, it is vigorous.

The music sounds again.

Malodorous lunchroom whores.

Lobster King

What time is it? It's 2:30 pm already? I must have slept for eleven hours.

I sleeken My hair with brilliantine.

In My dreams, a herd of naked old men chased Me through waving rows of corn, their withered penises slapping their bellies as they ran.

I walk softly from the Crystalline Hotel to Lobster King.

The grass-stalks are bespattered with crystalline dew from the evening downpour.

A psuedopod of liquefacient drips from the sky and onto My eyebrow.

Crustaceans creep through the deep, rain-wettened grass.

Rain-splotches decorate My tweed jacket. They come down in heavy beads, matting My hair.

Lobster King is a place where rainbows never shine.

Lobster King welcomes Me generously.

I walk into Lobster King and see happy sea creatures dancing in a tank full of verdant fluid.

Octopi and hydras with lit, burgeoning eyes gyrate in the tank. Their soft, moist, quivering tentacles embrace each other.

On a slick rock, mirthful crabs hop up and down mirthfully.

Lobsters gather in a large mass of dirty antennae and sharp claws; they hobble over each other busily. Their mouths expand and close rhythmically.

A viridescent fungus spreads over the slick rock.

Above the aquarium is a sign that reads: LOBSTER KING IS FULL OF HAPPY SURPRISES!

I jitterbug through the crowded lobby.

Someone behind Me says, "Too much masturbation can do straaaaaaaaaaaaaaaaaaange things to a man ... I have a friend back in East Iowa ... His penis was so hard that you could use it to jimmy open a window ... You know what happened to him? They found his legs twisted around his head. Like a mouse in a food processor."

The maître d' approaches Me and asks in a winsome voice, "How many in your party, sir?"

I don't know what she looks like because I'm not looking at her. I try not to think of the bloody tampon between her legs.

I say, "Table for one."

"Table for one" is code for "a table situated far away from everyone else."

Whenever you say the words, "Table for one" to the maître d', you are almost certainly guaranteed the most secluded table in the entire restaurant. Except tonight. There is a couple at the table next to Mine.

I try desperately to avoid meeting their eyes. Perhaps I can ask the waitress for a partition.

I quickly order the lobster thermidor. I will dine and depart. The waitress tells Me that Lobster King is a populist establishment and does not offer lobster thermidor. I order the lobster pâté instead, while glancing quickly at the table beside Me.

At the neighboring table are a tenuous-fingered young man and a beefy German *Schlampe*. They watch Me watching them. I watch them watching Me. What in dog's name do they want? They beckon.

The young man extends his slender fingers, welcoming Me into his welcoming arms. He reminds Me of a student I once taught in graduate school who had a predilection for onion dip.

Cocking his head up and down rooster-like, his throat bobbing obscenely, he inquires, "Excuse me sir would you like to join us at our table I mean."

"No, that's quite all right."

"Well I see you here sitting by yourself and I says to my wife he really looks lonely why don't you dine with us? I can see that you're alone. Come on and be friendly with us. We can have friendly fun!"

The young man waves his hands as if they were flapping flippers.

Lonely? That word has no meaning to Me. I am always alone but never lonely. Loneliness is a feeling that I have never experienced.

Only the feeble are lonely. Only the lonely are feeble. Solitude is the preferred state of being.

I have no choice but to join them. Even if I remain at My table, they will still try to engage Me in conversation.

I will impale them with words.

I say in a dim monotone, "Hello, My name is Jonathan Barrows."

The young man presents himself. A milky film coats the lobster appendages on his plate.

"I'm Brian. This is my wife Beate. We got married two months ago didn't we hon?"

I say unblinkingly to the German woman's diadem-shaped hairdo, "I am deeply sorry to hear that."

Marriage is the destruction of the individual ego.
— Jonathan Barrows

The German woman says, her lardlike teats quivering, "You are dressed so darkly, Mr. Barrows. Do you always wear dark colors?"

I say quasi-gently, "Perhaps My colors are lucent. Perhaps your eyes are too dim to see them."

While they speak to each other about somethingorother, I think of the autopsy that I carried out on the oyster in Ye Olde Diner.

"Beate and I were discussing the abortion issue since she's a woman of course Beate supports a woman's right to choose as she should there are only a few female pro-lifers. I'm pretty much a sensitive nineties kind of guy and so I support a woman's right to choose everyone should be pro-choice are you pro-choice too."

"No."

The young man sighs and draws back aggressively, as if he were an asp readying to strike. His teeth scintillate, envenomed with rage. I can see the poison circulating through the veins of his eye-globes.

My eyes dive into his own, unsettling the pleasant illusions that he has of himself.

"Well that's fine one of the things that makes this country so great is the diversity of opinion everyone has the freedom to speak his mind difference is good you must be pro-life then that's perfectly fine."

"No."

The young man looks at Me venomously and with visible consternation.

"Well, where do you stand in relation to the abortion issue?"

"I am pro-abortion."

While he speaks, he frowns at his dish: a shrimp pancake smothered with lobster velouté. His throat is glutted with fragments of crab flesh. A globe of light circles his head.

"Pro-abortion what do you mean no one in their right mind actually *supports* abortion. I see you're just

speaking in a farcical way ha ha ha really seriously though abortion is a choice that no woman wants to make it's almost certainly traumatic for her but nonetheless it's her body and who is a man to tell her what ..."

As he speaks, sparks of disgust invade My sense reactors. His mind is a rotting potato.

Young women should be encouraged to get pregnant and abort their fetuses.
— Jonathan Barrows

Most attempts to engage My attention fail. If the subject of a conversation is not Myself or selfhood in general, I lapse into a state of complete autism.

To divert Myself, I think of My beautifully flowing testicular hair.

The young man says somethingorother. I am not listening; whatever he is saying will have been forever blotted out of consciousness.

Chit-chat chit-chat.

Seemingly irritated by My mutism, the young man glares at Me.

He says bitterly and with unearned archness, "You know it is customary for people to talk to each other when they're sitting at the same table."

With well-earned archness, I say to his glass of Perrier, "Someday you will be pressed into mush by the tires of an eighteen-wheeled truck loaded with frozen cartons of banana ice cream."

He looks at Me, a prod-stunned cow.

My pâté arrives, a fat sponge delicately garnished with a delectable lobster/mushroom cream and sprinkled with Limburger crumbs.

The German woman wonders what My testicular hair looks like.

Her cheeks puff and hollow.

She says, "Brian is such a sweetie. He tells me every day that I am every man's fantasy."

She grimaces broadly, a sickeningly wide grin. Her lipstick resembles face paint.

The young man is, more likely, someone who flatters his wife in order to gain constant access to her vagina.

His sweat-glistened body vibrates as he spears the pinkish fold.

With a scathing leer on My face, I say to the wall behind her, "A fantasy? Yes, to a certain extent, that is true. You are, as it were, an oasis of the mind — but an oasis that neither promises nor yields refreshment."

The eggs in the incubator of her mind are beginning to hatch. With glossy eyes, the young man cranes his neck toward Me as if he were readying his jaws to bark.

His clammy face flaps.

He says sniffishly and snappishly, "Listen mister know-it-all that's my wife and don't you insult her. Your arrogance is really arrogant. I can tell that you're smart and all but you're not the only smart person in Benton Harbor."

I point My fork at the young man as if he were an unfresh shrimp that must be sent back to the kitchen.

I say fiercely, without looking at him, "The more that you attempt to offend Me, the more you affirm My

infinite superiority. You are nothing more than the agog spectator of My greatness. You germinated from the womb of a gray-haired feline. Your mother is an undomesticated cat, loose in the wild. You decanted milk from her heated breasts."

His face flattens.

The German woman's eyes simmer with contempt and unsated desire. *I can smell her musty vulva.* I gag and snort. Her vaginal perfume fumigates My nostrils.

She says to My virile shoulders, "Why don't you leave, sir? You have crossed a line."

Her carmine lips open and close.

I point My spoon at the German woman as if she were a wasp squirming in a bowl of *crème anglaise.*

I say without looking at her, "Do you know what I call German women?"

Gazing at My lush eyelashes, she asks with legible surprise, "What, then?"

"*Holeins.* Get it?"

The German woman shoots a glance at Me, gunning Me down with angry eyes.

I place a twenty-dollar greenback on the table and leave with dispatch.

I burst out of Lobster King and briskly race down Impression Avenue without looking back. If I were to turn around, I would dissolve into granules of powder.

Watch out.

Above Me flicker the leathery wings of a blackbird. The sun-stained pavement welcomes My advancing footfalls.

I love Myself. I love Myself. I love Myself. I love Myself. I love Myself. I love Myself. I love Myself. I love

*Myself. I love Myself. I love Myself. I love Myself. I love

Myself. I love Myself. I love Myself. I love Myself. I love
Myself. I love Myself. I love Myself. I love Myself. I love
Myself.*

The solar bladder has been decanted.

Someone — I think it was the French writer Georges
Bataille — composed a prose poem entitled "The Solar
Anus." I haven't read the work, but if he is comparing
the sun to an anus, then his analogy is
dissymmetrical.

The sun does not resemble the anus. No.

The sun is like the scrotum.

Droplets of sunlight are droplets of semen.

I dash into the Crystalline Hotel. I reach My hotel
room and enter the lavatory. I turn on the faucet, cup
My hands, and douse My face with hotel water.

Coils of hotel water unspool over My chalky arms in
hyalescent snakelike streams.

The Defenestration of the Inflatable Love Doll

I swim laps in the Crystalline Hotel's swimming pool. The water is warm and clear. The lifeguard stares at My buttocks as they shimmer beneath the surface of the water. I emerge from the depths and climb out of the pool, My hands propped on the edge. The cleft of My buttocks is slightly visible. I trail the pool's walkway until I reach the diving platform. I spring from the diving board and penetrate the water in a clean arc. The water hisses and fizzes around Me in distending circles. Shadows wrinkle the pool's smooth floor. Surfacing, I run My fingers through the tendrils of My thick hair. I lift Myself out of the water and dry My shoulders, chest, and back with a white towel.

Beams of light play upon the surface of the water. I squeeze out of the swimming pool area and ooze into the concourse. Globules of water trickle down My chest.

I commandeer the elevator to the third floor. I mince down the corridor to My hotel room, the towel slung smartly over My right shoulder.

As I shift into the room, dripping and cold, I notice that My window is gaping. The curtains balloon and flap. I look out the window. On the grass below lies sprawled My inflatable love doll. Someone pushed My double out the window.

Dazzlingly, I climb down the back staircase, push open the hotel door, and walk speedily to the back of the building. Water droplets glisten on My chest. The sun hurts My eyes. The tall blades of grass dance back and forth.

I see My double buried in the deep grass, moistened by a revolving garden sprinkler. I touch its grooved skin. Tears blear My eyes. The inflatable doll is deflated.

Its once bloated muscles have shrunken to strands of soft tissue.

I elevate the doll and hold it, sagging and soggy, against My chest. Motes of light glitter in its/My/our eyes.

I worm My way back into the Crystalline Hotel, stunned by the defenestration of the inflatable love doll.

Will the Interview Never Take Place?

It is time for My ablution. I jump into the shower stall with a bottle of Avocado-Banana Body Wash. The spumy lotion streams down My chest and back. Shower mist elevates and envelops My body. I manipulate My perineus muscle until My penis shoots up and greets My chin.

With elegance and style, I spring out of the lavatory. I dance in front of the mirror, swaying to unheard music. I smear pomade into My massive pompadour and stare lovingly at My lusciously naked body in the mirror.

Watch out.

I hear the sound of water boiling and the whirring of angry insects.

Someoneorother slipped a note underneath My door.

Only the lonely are feeble.

I pick up the note and read the following words, which are inscribed in orange ink:

RESPONDING AND WHAT THAT MEANS

The wind responds.
It responds by whispering into the wall of the barn.
The fox, too, responds.
It responds by sauntering around the trunk of the yew tree.
The yew tree responds.
It responds by molting its leaves.
The little girl responds.

> She responds by dancing in the leaves shed by the yew tree.
> The piece of paper responds.
> It responds by circling in the cool autumn air.
> The piece of paper responds.
> The little girl responds.
> The yew tree responds.
> The fox responds.
> The wind responds.
> You do not respond.

Unsure of what the text means, I tear the note into small bits and throw them into the rubbish bin. What flapdoodle! At least Saint Max is clear. *Der Einzige und sein Eigenthum* is the only readable book in the history of German philosophy. *Rothwelsch und Kauderwelsch.*

How I hate the incomprehensible!

I whirl through the corridors of the Benton Harbor Community College until I reach the office of the School of Learning.

The room is windowless; I never noticed that before.

Postured arm-on-hip and inhaling a Styrofoam cup weighted with caffeinated sewage water, Miss Grimmlager smiles emptily as I enter the darkened space.

Behind her looms a tower of Styrofoam cups. I will interrogate her. Ask her direct questions. That is the only way to find out what is going on.

I ask her bluntly, "Will the interview *never* take place?"

"Whose interview? Yours, Mr. Barrows?"

"Yes, My interview. Will My interview never take place?"

"Hasn't Dr. Mendoza contacted you yet?"

"No, Dr. Mendoza has not contacted Me, yet. Did you not tell him that I was staying at the Crystalline Hotel?"

"Yes, Mr. Barrows, I did tell him that."

"When?"

"Two days ago."

"And what did he say? How did he respond?"

"To what?"

"How did he respond when you told him that I would be staying at the Crystalline Hotel?"

"He didn't say anything. He nodded. He took the information in and nodded."

"Did he acknowledge that he knew who I was?"

"No. Unless the nod was a form of acknowledgment. But that nod could have also merely been a sign of indifference and boredom. Perhaps he didn't know who you were. Perhaps he wasn't listening. Perhaps he only nodded to appease me."

"Miss Grimmlager, what *exactly* did you say to him?"

"I told him that a Mr. Barrows came by for an interview. I also told him that you'd be staying at the Crystalline."

"And he said *nothing*?"

"As I told you, Mr. Barrows, he nodded, and that was it."

"Miss Grimmlager, is Dr. Mendoza here now?"

"No, Mr. Barrows, although, as I told you, he'll be teaching a seminar Monday evening. He only has one teaching responsibility this summer."

"May I speak to the Director of the School of Learning?"

"If you'd like, but she has nothing to do with your interview or the hiring process. The position for which

Joseph Suglia

you applied, Professor of Intelligent Thinking, is the province of Dr. Mendoza and him alone."

Her whisper-thin eyebrows connecting, Miss Grimmlager stuffs a glazed doughnut into her mouth.

She champs and then speaks. Her eyes dim as she articulates words.

"You know, Mister Dainty Shoes, you look very much like that actor."

The frustration rising in My voice, I ask her, "*Which* actor?"

"You know, that actor. What's his name? Just a minute."

Sitting upright, Miss Grimmlager draws an invisible chimpanzee with her hands.

"Let me think. Who is he?"

"I know," she suddenly exclaims as she throws the half-extinguished doughnut into the rubbish barrel. "Jude Law. That's it. You look just like that Jude Law."

The words sprout from her mouth like massive vines.

"Excuse Me, Madam, but I certainly do not resemble Jude Law. Mr. Law, however, may bear a slight resemblance to ME."

Like everyone else in Benton Harbor, Michigan, this woman is incompetent and cannot be relied upon to do anything. The residents of this town are like useless children stranded in a world of dutiful adults.

Because they always disappoint, they never disappoint.

Why should I hope to receive a meaningful answer from her? All of this blabbering about popular culture. I must assume a more direct approach.

I will pursue Dr. Mendoza's tracks. I will attend the seminar.

Miss Grimmlager looks at Me vapidly and asks, "Do you enjoy looking at my hair? Do you enjoy its wavy curls?"

Miss Grimmlager spreads her shoulder blades expansively and then suddenly retracts, withdrawing deep into her ultra-big chair.

Seized with an urgent desire for a strong cup of java, I remove a cup from the Styrofoam tower. All of the white cups hail noisily to the ground.

Watch out.

Her pinned-open eyes agape, Miss Grimmlager starts and gasps. She recedes more deeply into her chair. Bulbous, her burgeoning eyes threaten to spurt out of their eye-holes. Her fingers tense and tighten. Her body shakes in violent palpitations. Her lips grow terse. Her face expands.

Suddenly, a jet of orange foam spews from her mouth. A gigantic orange puddle extends across the desk, wetting the desk things. The spumy orange cascades over the edge of the desk in mini-waterfalls; the foam sprays onto the carpet in splattering rushes. Droplets of orange drip from her drooping eyebrows.

A new spout emerges from the darkness of her insides. The violent orange stream propulsively emanates across the room. Meaty chunks of orange vomit fly everywhere, flooding the office. The orange foam spurts from her mouth in heavy flows. She tilts her head back; the geyser surges upward. It propels from her mouth and strikes the ceiling and falls back down again in a shower of orange. The fountain of spume gushes across the floor of the office.

Joseph Suglia

My hands shielding My face, I weave out of the office backwards, squealing with thick disgust.

I do not understand Miss Grimmlager's bizarre behavior.

I do not understand why I have not yet been interviewed.

I do not know where Dr. Mendoza is.

I do not understand why Dr. Mendoza has not yet telephoned Me.

I do not understand why I am here.

I do not understand why everyone in Benton Harbor is seemingly deranged. Is it the water?

I search the file cabinet of My mind for an explanation that would clarify this muddle.

The files are empty.

Becoming a Man

In the summer of My eighteenth year, My parents assigned to Me a lady-friend.

They were troubled by the fact that I showed no interest in members of the opposite gender.

A professor of psychology at the University of Toledo, My sister, said, "He must be suffering from some aberrant strain of sexual anaesthesia."

My parents resolved to initiate Me in the ways of the flesh.

They walked proudly to the house of our neighbors, the Barnhams. I trailed behind them.

Ascending the concrete steps, My father pounded on the front door. My mother collared My neck so that I could not escape.

Mr. Barnham, who wore a bright pink polo shirt, opened the door magnanimously and greeted My parents.

"Hi, I'm Teddy Barrows, and this is my wife, Norine. You know us, don't you? We live three doors down. Ours is the house with the swing set in the front yard."

Placing her hands firmly around My neck, My mother said, throttling Me, "Johnny is our boy! Johnny just loves to play on the swings, don't you, Johnny?"

"Well then," Mr. Barnham said. "What can I do for you?"

"We were wondering if you would allow your daughter, Bernice to court our son. They both go to Herberger together, and we think they'd make a darling pair. She has an ample bosom but is not overly attractive. Remember what W. B. Yeats said about his baby girl: *Let her be good-looking but not too good-looking.*

Joseph Suglia

"Has Bernice been deflowered yet? And does she have any physical deformities?"

"Let me see, now," said Mr. Barnham, his brow corrugating. He bellowed up the staircase, "BERNICE!"

Out of the shadows bounced a young female. Mr. Barnham gripped her around the neck and pulled her into the doorway.

"Damned kids. You've got to know how to handle them."

Her ruddy lips spreading across her face, My mother cackled through her yellow teeth, spitting out a glob of phlegm with each cackle.

"All-righty," said Mr. Barnham. "What was the first requirement?"

Drawing out each syllable with violence, My mother asked, "Has she been deflowered?"

Mr. Barnham asked his daughter, "Bernice, has any boy ever stuck his thing inside of you?"

She tightened her lips and said nothing.

"Bernice, I asked you a question. Did any boy ever put his thingamajig inside of you?"

She did not respond.

"Fucking bitch!" the father cried and pushed his daughter to the ground.

His hairy, tattooed arm seized a black umbrella, drawing it out of its native canister. He spun the umbrella around his head in an ever-widening circle. It circled in the air, whistling as it spun.

The umbrella struck the ceiling. Bits of white plaster rained down on his daughter's cowering head. It plummeted through space and smashed against her legs.

"Take that, you fucking bitch! And that! And that!"

Bernice yelped as the umbrella repeatedly crashed down on her kneecaps. She yielded to the razor-deep

100

blows. Mr. Barnham pounded on his daughter's back with the umbrella as she writhed in agony; but she did not resist him.

"And that! And that! You fucking bitch! I'm the king! I'm the master! You fucking bitch! You won't control me! I'm the king! You will obey me! You fucking bitch! I run the show around here! I bring home the bacon! You fucking bitch! You fucking bitch! I work hard for the money, you fucking bitch!"

The entire house shook with his fury. With every blow, a cataclysm vibrated throughout the neighborhood.

Bernice was a sobbing, whimpering animal that did nothing to shield the shocks that thundered against her body.

The hail of blows hammered down upon her harder and then stopped.

"There," the father said, panting with excitement. "Fucking bitch. That will show her that I'm the boss around here. From now on, she'll do what I say, when I say it. Fucking cunt ... What was the question again?"

As the daughter huddled together weeping, her soft arms cradling her skinless bloodied kneecaps, My mother smiled and asked, "Is she a virgin?"

Bernice murmured and squirmed.

"Well," Mr. Barnham said. "I certainly never had sexual intercourse with my own daughter, if that's what you mean ... I never even touched her down there. OK, I did, but only once, and that was just to make sure that her hymen was still intact. But that was me, her father, doing that and not the milkman or God knows who else. I'm her father, and I have the right to touch my daughter if I goddamn please. She needed a gynecological examination, and we got one for free."

My father scribbled on a stenographic pad and said quietly, as if to himself, "I suppose since it occurred within the confines of the family ... it's fine."

Mr. Barnham said in a slightly irritated tone, "Anything else on the menu? What's next? Does she have pubic hair?"

My father said disapprovingly, "Oh no, Mr. Barnham. We are not sick, uncouth people. Just a few more questions ... Is she intelligent?"

"Hell, no, she's as dumb as a lemming."

"We can see that she is semi-attractive. Wouldn't you agree, darling?"

"Yes, she's rather pretty but not overly pretty. Very large mammary glands."

"Does she have at least one physical deformity?"

"She has scars from head to toe. I made sure of that. She has a drill hole burrowed into the side of her head, too. I don't know how it got there. She must have done it to herself. Fucking bitch ..."

That is how our courtship began.

We "dated" — if that is the right word — every Sunday afternoon from June until late August.

On the day of what would be our final meeting, I sauntered to the Barnhams' and rapped semi-softly on their front door, while My parents observed My movements through a telescope. Mr. and Mrs. Barnham invited Me inside and forced biscuits down My throat.

After thirty-five minutes had passed, Bernice and I tracked the sidewalk until we reached the house of My parents. They chatted with her until the conversation swirled into a gaping abyss.

Bernice and I then sat silently on the sofa in the living room for one hour.

She wore the same orange-tinted sunglasses that she always wore on Sunday afternoons.

Her lips were glistening strawberry protuberances.

To freshen her up for our date, Mrs. Barnham cut Bernice's hair two hours prior to our assignation. She placed a sieve over Bernice's head and sheared off the hair that exceeded the metallic perimeter with a pair of sewing shears.

Bernice wore a ruffled yellow dress. The word, "Sunday" was embroidered over her left breast.

Her cheeks twitched roughly every five minutes. To pass the time, I timed the periodic twitching of her cheeks with My stainless-steel Nietzsche wristwatch.

She folded her hands demurely on her right knee, as her mother instructed her to. My boredom surpassed all limits.

"Bernice," I said suddenly. "Let us go walking through the park, shall we?"

Bernice complied emotionlessly.

I strolled through the park, indifferent to the young woman who strolled beside Me.

I was abstracted, disengaged, as if I were in another place, infinitely distant from the role that was imposed upon Me.

Before us was an elderly man with opaque sunglasses.

The elderly man strutted down the walkway toward a flock of checkered gulls.

The birds were motionless, squatting on the pavement.

A daemonic grimace widened on the elderly man's wrinkled face.

He unsheathed a serpentine cord. With a single sweep of the whip, a gull flopped on its side, bloodred. Cracks and snaps resounded through the air. The

elderly man mutilated the gulls remorselessly, but with vigor and passion.

He massacred the defenseless animals in order to strengthen his grip on the convulsions that fomented within his own body.

Withdrawing behind a many-feathered yew tree, Bernice cringed and stifled her wet screams.

"Stranger," I said, approaching the elderly man, who had provoked himself into a froth. "Why are you destroying these bonny creatures?"

The elderly man did not deign to answer My question.

The gulls did not take flight; nor did they attempt otherwise to escape their chastisement. They never squawked. They lined up in a disorderly row, steeled to all fear, and prepared themselves for their impending slaughter at the hands of the man with the whip. In a somnambulistic daze, the gulls trotted toward their deaths.

I returned to My parents' home and fondled My penis until a thick, glutinous substance spewed out of its mouth.

The "Bernice affair," as it came to be known, had repercussions in My household, as well as that of the Barnhams.

After the incident, Bernice fell into a deep stupor, suffered violent cataleptic fits, and chewed most of her fingernails off.

My parents despaired at finding Me a mate; nonetheless, they were determined to, as they put it, "deflower Me."

They spent good money to have My virginity removed.

Wearing wide-brimmed hats, dark sunglasses, and gray trench-coats, My mother and father trawled the

city's red-light district in search of a prostitute for their wayward son.

Leaning against the loading gate of a sausage factory was a woman-for-hire named Margaret. "Margaret" was, in fact, merely the procuress's nom d'amour. She was a Polish immigrant and Prozac addict who used men for money, antidepressants, and possible citizenship.

Like most prostitutes, she bore a blank face. Her blank face uttered words that contradicted its own vacant expression.

On the day My parents brought Me a Polish prostitute, I was lying in My bed reading My Ovid.

I glanced at My self-portrait, which hung beside the mirror above My dresser. My bedsheets were littered with unfresh puddles of coagulated semen. Gluey stalactites of semen dangled from the ceiling.

I heard My mother calling Me through the intercom.

I said into the intercom, "Come up, Mother! I'll undo the lock!"

My bedroom door had a combination lock, although My parents knew the password. I arched to the door and undid the lock.

My parents coached Me in the art of loving. They wanted Me to have sexual intercourse with the Polish prostitute.

They tugged two lawn chairs up the staircase and pulled them next to My bed.

My father exclaimed, "Showtime in five minutes!"

They sat on the lawnchairs. Between them was a stool. Upon the stool was propped a bowl of freshly baked popcorn.

My mother ejaculated, "Get ready!"

Margaret traipsed into My bedroom, a cigarette dangling from her full lips, and leaned against My

dresser. She was fully dressed in the garb of a demure young woman.

Margaret drew in the breath of the cigarette, exhaled plumes of smoke through her arched nostrils, and said, "So you just want me to have sex with him, right? Not you two, as well? ... I mean, if you want me to have sex with all three of you at once, that's fine, but I'm going to need at least two grand more for that. Incest costs extra."

My mother smiled politely and said in a calm voice, "We want you break him in, dear, that's all."

She happily waved a handmade flag upon which were emblazoned the words: "GO, JOHNNY, GO!"

The words were mimeographed in Day-Glo orange.

Brandishing a videocamera, My father screamed, "Come on, Johnny! Get ready!"

I walked to the family water closet and silently undressed in the dimly lit space.

I emerged, wearing nothing other than My monogrammed bathrobe and duck slippers, and threaded the long corridor that led to My bedroom.

My footfalls slapped the wooden floor. Crestfallen, I paced slowly and solemnly into My bedroom.

As My parents cheered Me on, I climbed onto My bed and removed My garment. I didn't want to remove My duck slippers.

Widening his mouth as if he were a bovine farm animal in the act of giving birth, My father bellowed. Words issued from his spreading mouth, "Let's get ready to rumble!"

Gesturing wildly at Margaret, he trumpeted, "Look at your mate! Go on! Stare at his masculinity! Go on! Go on!"

With *faux* modesty, Margaret raised her eyes to My youthful nakedness. Like a trained actress, she

expertly imitated the callow ways and gestures of a nymph unschooled in amour. She examined My bulge for what seemed to be a miniature eternity, her eyes deepening into bottomless sinkholes.

I shivered with grief. I could feel her cold, probing, slime-mucked eyeballs roll over My supple chest.

She laughed musically, her hair bouncing across her face as she ululated.

No longer affecting reserve, she stripped off her sweater, thrusting out the clothed domes of her breasts. She swayed hypnotically back and forth, unbuttoning her blouse slowly and rhythmically.

As she undulated, My parents clapped to the rhythm of her funky beat.

I groaned in misery.

Each button of Margaret's blouse popped, bursting open, displaying more and more skin. She unabashedly stared at My penis as she tore open her blouse. As she gazed at My horrified gaze, she chuckled, pushing her pelvis forward obscenely. She clasped her hands behind her back and unlatched her black brassiere with deliberate slowness.

Rose-hued areolae surrounded her arrow-shaped nipplistic analysis staring conspicuously interlocking eye-pupils salient breasts snuggled by the luster of a whisper-thin conical brassiere perking obnoxiously through its translucent waves like an enormous pair of slippery rancid unshelled eggs; a glimpse at her two bulging mammary glands would make a normal man salivate but Jonathan Barrows is not a normal man to him they were merely protuberances consisting of rank adipose tissue that belonged on a farm animal rather than on a human animal. Breasts like breakers against a bursting dam, raging sea.

She pulled off her brassiere gradually until her fleshy, jiggling white globes popped out. The shivering globes spooned into My mouthing-range, their nubs twitching like the pink noses of rabbits.

Nodding in fervent admiration, My father said, "Damn, she's good! You should get you a job at the White Leopard, honey!"

Margaret bounded onto My paralyzed body, pressing the burgeoning softness of her chest into My resisting visage.

Unveiling a disposable still camera, My mother flashed four quick shots for the family album.

Margaret's grin widened.

"That's my Johnny! Stick it in there, boy! Don't be a coward!"

Margaret slithered her hand gently down My chest until it reached My unthrusting sex.

I screamed. I could do nothing.

Her lips coupled and parted, unified and divided like viscous butterflies.

"Come on, Johnny! Fuck her, my boy! Use the cock that God gave you! What do you think it's there for? Chicken hunting? Do it, already!"

"Rip those underpants off, dear! Right this instant!"

Margaret exposed her puberulent pucker. She unhusked and unshelled, her mind tunneling through the airy realm of insubstantial spectres.

Masticating noisily, My mother champed the popcorn.

She exhorted, "Give her a kiss, Johnny! Be decent!"

Margaret came at Me with flaying windmill-arms.

"Hey, listen, son!" said My father. "When I gave it to your mother the first time, there was plenty o' foreplay.

Why don't you do the same? A girl like this doesn't come around every day! Don't blow it, son!"

Margaret licked her lips, pulsating violently to soundless music. She tousled the billows of her ashen hair. She slid silkily over My nakedness and warmed My chest with her gelid hands. Her hands scythed through the luxuriating meshes of My pubic hair.

"Give it a shot, boy! Take her for a ride! Straddle that filly! Make her suffer! Show her who's boss!"

My mother's mouth spewed forth the words, "Stroke those thighs, honey!"

Raising herself from the lawnchair, My mother approached the bed.

"Here, I'll show you."

She palmed and stroked and simonized and massaged Margaret's generously flowing hips.

Margaret spit out, "Hey, Mom, I said that multiple partners'd be extra!"

My mother said to My face, which was distorted in agony, "Don't you like girls, Johnny darling?"

"All right, son," My father said, "this is where we separate the men from the boys."

Margaret moaned sonorously and clenched her fists. She lashed Me with her hair and her body. I pulled My pelvis backward. My father whirled around the bed, focusing the video camera on Margaret's grinding hips.

"That's it! Did you see that? I've got to get a shot from that angle!"

"Rear those hips, Johnny!"

A thick skin spread over My eyes and congealed. My face grew clammy. Her vixenish eyes studied the contortions of My face. I studied the pustules on her nose.

Joseph Suglia

Cries of lust germinated from her mouth. She tried to jell her body with My own, but My penis would not stand.

Her vulva moistened. Her labia were ready to osculate. I could feel their wine-dark touch. But My penis would not stand. It would not insert itself into her tubuscular cavity.

"Come on, Mister Wishy-Washy!"

Her vagina yielded, but My penis resisted.

Our bodies would not conglutinate.

Around My bed, My mother and father pounded on the bedsheets and cheered Me on.

"Stick it in her, boy!"

"Mount that Pole!"

"Mount that Pole!"

"Mount that Pole!"

"Impale her!"

Intermission

Some of you may be wondering why I am so cool.
A pointed question.
The reason is that I am Jonathan Barrows.

Watch out.

I desire no one besides Myself.
And I am the object of everyone's love.
There is no one else like Me in the world.
And I am the greatest you'll ever see.
Once I disappear from the world, no one else will supplant Me.
You should feel privileged to read My words.
Photocopy My journal. Disseminate copies among your close friends and kin. This is My body. By reading Me, you are affirming the greatness of Jonathan Barrows.
Those who encircle Me are My creations, My property, things of use. You, too, My reader, are My creation, My property, a thing that I may use, if it pleases Me.
You are welcome.

I unopen My eyes and imagine that I am lying supine on the floor of an abandoned classroom, incapable of moving My arms or legs.
A black space stretches around Me. My mouth widens into a voiceless scream.
If My body were to liquefy, how would I differentiate between My thoughts and the things of the world?
All those whom I encounter stare up in wonderment at the unobtainable reaches of My greatness.
I am a lightning rod for all of the world's desire.
But no one is My light-of-love.
I magnetize every creature within a two-mile radius.
But I would rather repel them.
Every man and woman I meet is entrained into My private sphere.

But I want to preserve the sacredness of My solitude.
They want to poke their flashlights inside of Me. They
want to grip Me in their coils.
For I am made a dark and incomprehensible figure.

A man of exquisite beauty, the Prince wanders through the
grove that lies behind the Crystalline Hotel. The wind rushes
through the meshes. His lithe ankles, his august forehead,
his erect purple nipples, his cold pale-blue irises, his
fluttering mouth, his lithe neck, his golden shoulders, his
thick lips, the full waves of his long, ever-umbrellaing
eyelashes, his explosive blonde mane, his segmented chest
— all of these things sparkle, fire, flare, burst, and glisten.
He is absolutely vibrant. Perhaps it is this vibrancy that
draws the residents of Benton Harbor, Michigan, into his life-
sphere. Perhaps it is his difference from the collective.
Perhaps it is his supreme self-possessedness. Who can say?
All that is certain is that the Prince is the ideal man. A man
unlike any other man.
The Prince cups his filmy arms into a parabola and
balances on a single, well-toned leg. He leaps from one rock
to another as the spectators gasp at his balletic agility.
Mist envelops the marshland.
The moorfowl cackle.
No one knows who the Prince is.
But he is all-knowing.
Someday, the Prince will swallow himself.
Consumed, he will be as mute as stone.

Why do they desire Me? What is this force of attraction,
this irresistible magnetism? What does desire desire?
Desire desires desire.
Das Mögen mag die Möglichkeit.
Desire desires what comes out and withdraws at the
same time.
Desire is drawn to that which protrudes.
Penises thrusting forward arrogantly. Bulging breasts.
Nipples piercing sweat-stained T-shirts. Pronounced biceps.
Swelling buttocks. Bulbous testicles. A perineum showing

112

conspicuously through a bright orange leotard. A tangle of spider-black pubic hair. Prominent body parts lead human beings astray.

What is seductive *bursts* out.

Think of breasts — I prefer not to — coming loose from their lacy containers. Or penises that are so humungous that they break free from the constraint of their vanilla codpieces.

My muscles jut through My open-collared silk shirt, driving Me into a state of delirium.

When I snake down the corridor of the Crystalline Hotel, My gluteus maximus shimmies, extruding rudely through My perfectly pleated trousers. My testicles burgeon forth. My serpentine love-tentacle throbs ostentatiously. It, too, protrudes. My body moves protrusively as it walks.

Watch out.

I am a steaming mound of sensuality. No one will ever have Me. I alone reap the harvest of My inexpressible beauty.

I am not merely beautiful; I am *transcendentally* beautiful. Is this the force, is this the irreversible magnetism that draws human beings into My world? On the one hand, My natural attractiveness draws spectators into My sphere. On the other hand, human beings desire Me because *I am desired by others.*

Desire is not merely geared toward an object.
Desire is geared toward the desire that surrounds that object.
— Jonathan Barrows

The more I am desired by others, the more desirable I become. My indifference, too, leads them astray. The absence of desire attracts desire to itself. Most are swayed by My *ataraxia*, My imperturbable calm.

My self-subsistence perturbs them. I am impossibly self-sufficient. For this reason, I incite desire. For this reason, I

Joseph Suglia

excite envy. My attractiveness is multidimensional. I am preternaturally fine.

Wherever I go, young girls gaze at Me with a thirst that will never be slaked.

I wander through the grove behind the Crystalline Hotel in Benton Harbor, Michigan. Two young lovers dance down a streamside lane. Their bodies are suffused in a mirage of buttermilk sunshine. The young lovers are two reflections of the same person.

That person is Jonathan Barrows.

Braids of water jet toward vorticular mouths.

I prance like a logroller over catatonic limbs of corrugated timber. Licking My eyelid sideways, I marvel at the unseen geometry of it all.

In the grove, there is no such thing as pubic hair.

I am surrounded by melting mirrors and images, transparent screens, disfigured surfaces, and glistening black beads. Braids of white fluid drip down the bark of the yew tree.

Whirling all around Me is the fecundating black, making oceans of inches and snail-sized gaps of wide voids.

The black writhes.

This is a sacred flaxfield of creeping nightmare love.

The heady air stenches beautifully of moss. It is enfragranted, as well, by My pungent man-musk.

Everywhere is tornado vomit.

Listen to the happy quacking of the nightinsects.

On the blanched whaleback rock lie wet flaps of partridge fat.

The black leaves are dripping.

The brittle leaves dance crisply in the frozen air.

All of these things are revealed to My gunning vision.

A lethargic muskhog buries its snout in the dark grass-bristles.

The night, it is luciferous.

The wild muskhogs bark menacingly as they skulk through the luscious herbage that covers the median strip.

114

An octogenarian mounts and straddles an equine tree, grasping its branches, using its hacked limbs as reins and spurs. Though the tree remains pedestrian, rooted in solid ground, the octogenarian gallops away merrily.

See the old man ride the tree.

The moon bobs into the firmament. Through the lunar candescence fly daemon-eyed lops.

The moon is a windy glint of phosphorescence in an open-ceilinged vicarage.

The clouds whorl around the moon's acne-ridden face. The moon's eye unopens and then uncloses again; it disappears from the space of the night.

On the beach sprawls a lamia in slime repose.

Excess litters the sky.

My penis is a gigantic brontosaurus. Godzilla-huge, it ejaculates its syrupy juices. I want tidal waves of semen to spew from My penis.

I want to deluge every diner in the world with My semen.

Watch out.

Sea worms come out of the waves to greet Me, smiling their mouthless smiles. They splash and jump into the air with merriment.

The clouds dissolve into jelly-coils.

A droplet of liquefacient drifts lacily through a pillow of air.

I wade through the plasmatic depths of the night.

Above Me dangle tightly knitted branches. The branches warp into mottles and splotches.

My mind unsheathes itself, whirling in a hurricane. Kaleidoscopic images spin rapidly in My brain.

This is where the wild worms sleep.

I see the women in scarlet bedclothes rise and exit the Crystalline Hotel. Their shrouds approach Me as I sail through the opaque night.

Earlier today, My neighbors gathered unhidden underneath My window. Some waded in the turgid gutters; others sat on logs. All wielded binoculars in their firm hands.

115

The binoculars aimed at the glass slate of My window, behind which I stood in disgust. I was perfectly visible and enlarged by their ever-present, magnifying vision.

Crests and breakers ascend into mountains of foam. Lake Michigan is not a lake, but an ocean. —

The emergence of the waves frightens Me. The emergence of the women frightens Me.

The crisp whispering of the yew trees sounds like angry brain cells.

The mind is volatile dispersal.

The slippery animals bask in the backwater fields. Their rows of sharp teeth resemble combs.

Everything is black now.

Feathery wisps speckle the moonless void.

Here is where the silent worms sleep.
The skin of the hotel throbs. The skin of the hotel pulsates.
Within the flesh, the flesh.

The stench of sex rises blackly like a cloud of wasps.

Summer is the time of fecundation.
Summer is the time of deterioration.
Summer is the time of sex.
Sex is fecundation.
Sex is deterioration.
Space fecundates.
Space deteriorates.
Sex whirls, spirals, pushes, and gushes.
Space speaks.
Everywhere is the fecundating of sex.
Everywhere is the deteriorating of sex.
Everywhere is fecundating of space.
Everywhere is the deteriorating of space.
I precipitate into the void of sex.
Summer is the time of space.
Summer is the time of sex.

Sex as crucifixion, sex as control, sex as mutilation, sex as humiliation, sex as blackmail, sex as tantalization, sex as a

sedative, sex as nausea, sex as emulsion, sex as disintegration.
I know the expansion of space.
I know the expansion of sex.
Sex is space.
Space is sex.

The Prince lies petrified on the floor of the classroom. He is forced to fix his stare on the sunless horizon. He recognizes that motion, dynamism, is impossible. Immobilized, he recognizes the futility of lifting a single arm, the absurdity of raising his eyes, the senselessness of voluntarily twitching his testicular sac, the pointlessness of smacking his red gums.
All movement is nullity, dead like a dead, wingless bird.
All is reduced to a static clarity, a formlessness, a neutrality that is the suspension of all activity. The surrounding atmosphere tightens against his body as if it were a sheet of transparent tissue.
Space spaces meat from bone. Space creates structures and configurations.
The air is itself a solid substance, without being perceptible as such.
What constitutes the putative necessity of motility? There is no need to move.
Activity is annihilation.
He senses the vibration, the motor activity, that is thought's.
Thought permutes itself in a hall of mirrors.
Thought reflects itself infinitely.
Movement is the absence of all change.
After contemplating the endless discourse of tree and sky, the Prince recognizes that there is no difference between his consciousness and the outside world; the surrounding ether is but an illusion.

When I awoke this morning, My body was wrapped in an alien skin. The enveloping skin was elastic and pliable. I sat on My bed and tore parts of the skin off with My fingernails.

117

Joseph Suglia

As I peeled away the diaphanous skin, I noticed that a subcutaneous layer subsisted beneath it. The sub-epidermis resembled phosphorescent mucous. I dug My fingernails deep into the layers of skin.

It struck Me that it was not a foreign skin that had wrapped itself around My body; rather, My own skin had transformed overnight into a milky and labile sheath. I plunged My fist into the skin, penetrating My flesh. Like a dam tested by the pressure of waves, My skin began to rupture. Through the yawning hole spewed a river of putrilaginous slime.

My fingers dove into the breach. I felt My intestines swimming around in My chassis. I groped My insides. I held My liver and passionately stroked My beautiful gall bladder.

I cradled the wad of viscera in My hands.

The wad mewed softly.

Within the flesh, the flesh.

Today, there is a street fair in Benton Harbor. The street, Impression Avenue, has been barricaded. The warden at the gate demands a toll.

Auf der Messe messen die Menschen Mich mit den Blicken.

Each fair-goer moves penumbrally through the turnstiles. They sinuate past Me, sometimes jostling Me with triangulated elbows. I wind My way through the broadening throng.

Towering above them, My body shades their own. The wrathful sun, it scintillates. The swarm, it is overpowering.

Wafting through the air is a faint but unmistakable scent, the acrid odor of horse dung.

Why am I here? Very often, at fairs, vendors hawk sex toys.

If I remain in Benton Harbor one more day, I will need to procure a well-oiled dildo.

I want to plunge My fist into My anus and finger the Braille of My inner life.

118

All around Me squirms a panorama of vulgar humanity.
The crowd breaks into files.
Crowds invade and liquefy. On the one hand, the crowd infiltrates and colonizes your body, making it its own. On the other hand, the crowd liquefies your body, melting it, until it coalesces with the viscous mass.
Once it reaches critical mass, the crowd takes on an identity that is radically distinct from the individuals who make it up.
The crowd has no order except that which it itself constitutes.
Stupidity is the intellectual disposition of the crowd. Stupidity is not a minute property, but a global problem, a viral contagion, a pestilential menace.
I see the fair-goers with their Burger God T-shirts. They are sunk into their own insignificance. Nothing is more averse to them than solitude. They attempt to flee from their solitude by squirming with others in the crowd. Their solitude increases, the more they dissolve into the crowd.
The fair-goers are pulverized, ground up into minute quantities, and then fed into the crowd-machine.
I zombie through the fanlike waves of the crowd.
I stare with contempt at a vendor who offers cotton candy to children. She feels her insignificance in relation to the immutable cosmos. She feels her mortality, an anguished forecast. Someday, her identity will be liquidated.
To balm the sense she has of her impending death, she envelops her husband's penis in the darkening evening.
Over the stones trample the ungular footfalls of horses. From the solitude of his booth, a hawker hawks equine glue-sap.
Everyone is immersed in the crowd. Crowd is like a spreading puddle. The crowd opens up like a fan. The crowd envelops Me. It radiates in all directions; its rows extend everywhere.
I am stung by electrified bodies.
The crowd fluidifies everything in its path. It is the making-liquid of everything fast and fixed.
Nothing solid can persist in the crowd's flood.

119

Joseph Suglia

Here, all that's done is undone.
A horse's angry maw slavers.

A magazine rack screams into My mute ears:
"A CAVALIER EXCLUSIVE: CINDY CRAWFORD UNWRAPPED — THE PICTURES YOU HOPED YOU'D NEVER SEE!"

A clerk swirls lemonade milkshakes in plastic cups; he hands them to the eager hands of his waiting clients.
Rude girls throw hoops over prongs, seemingly oblivious that they are rehearsing the act of copulation that they will perform with their cousins when the summer sun dallies in the sky.
Screeching children dangle from the cars of a Ferris wheel. The Ferris wheel is stalled. The children claw their faces and paw at each other, rabid with acrophobia.
The crowd spins, spirals, and wheels.

Someone behind Me yells into My ear:
"MOVE IT, MISTER TURKEY-COCK!"

A muscled troglodyte hoists a mallet over his shoulder and brings it down on a metallic scale. The scale quivers from the deadening impact.
The crowd umbrellas outward.
I drift past a booth within which are exhibited columns of paintings.
The sky ruptures; it is filigreed with sludge-tracks. Fluid spews from the celestial wound.
I behold the paintings. One shows a virgin straddling a slug as if it were a horse. Her eyes are turned upside-down. Her reversed eyes are blank white orbs. Another painting displays a face gradually melting into pudding. Behind the dissolving face is a yew tree. The antlers of the yew tree are draped with a gigantic white blanket. The woman behind the yew tree — she, too, is enshrouded in white.

120

A sperm whale ascending into the sky, its flippers flapping as it rises. The beak of the whale juts upward, permeating the frothing waves. Behind it, a ship.

The whale spirals into the air. Gigantic waves balloon and capsize around the ascending whaleflesh.

Its body sails ever-so slowly upward.

Flies dawdle around a dollop of plasmatic horse dung.

Doddering and slobbering, an old woman murmurs a language to herself that only she could understand. As I thrust My body forward, popcorn cracks under My feet.

A blasted landscape this will be.

The only person erect and breathing wandering through the worldless void.

Such overwhelming ugliness cannot be blotted out or contained. Self-murder? That would be a release. But then there would be no more I.

The world is a panorama of vulgarity.

An erogenous impulse incites Me, drives Me, prompts Me, irritates Me.

Somewhere in this infinite desert there is a dildo, and I will find it.

A regimented file of fair-goers mills into the exhibition center. I disdain to follow it.

An eager hand gropes Me. I turn around and see a guilty-faced young boy looking at Me guiltily.

Out of the boy's mouth fall the segmented scales of a shellfish.

I throw back My hand, ready to strike him. I think the better of it and slacken My fist.

I tramp through the rows of foul-smelling sludge that line the street, damp mixtures of horse faeces, cotton candy, and popcorn. My feet are steeped in the putrilage.

A puddle of slime shimmers with rays from the dead sun.

Veiling My eyes, I shift into an unpeopled stretch of tar.

The crowd fills up every open space.

I shield My body from the crowd's invading expanse.

I am sheathed in a sheet of flesh.

The thin sheet trembles.

The mob buzzes around Me.

A vast panorama of vulgar humanity, the mob spreads itself open.

I need a dark background in order to shine.

My luminescence shines brightly through the darkness. The mob is My backdrop. Its darkness illuminates Me, casting Me in relief.

My self is ever-expanding, infinitely moving outward.

The world exists for My benefit alone.

I step on the rank carcass of a partridge. Its eyes pour out of its tiny head and drop sightlessly onto the dusty street.

The crowd extends its lobes and nodes, pressing them into the recesses of the evening.

Before Me is an amusement park ride.

Its sign blazons:
"VULVA OF LOVE."

A mobile car drifts across the surface of a brown fluvius. It careens into the vulva-shaped orifice of a plastic cave. The pachydermic folds of the vulva have been sprayed with black paint.

A balmy zephyr fans My hair.

Wraiths and banshees spring out of the darkness. Sea-children enwreathed with kelp swirl and spiral among the waves. The riders blanch and squeal with fright. Their tongues unravel. Out of the cloacal abyss spits another car.

The crowd furls and then unfurls again.

I hear a harsh shout:
"YOUZE GOT A QUARTER!"
Another, behind it:
"I WAN COTTON CANDY!"

The untethered wind breezes through My mane.

The wind rends the sky into ribbons.

The wind shears the crowd, slicing it into discrete quantities.

A blunt shove comes from behind. Whose hand issued from the crowd's mouth? Dirty fucker.

Watch out.

I will place him into a stranglehold. I will compress his neck with anaconda hands. I will constrict his oxygen flow until he expires.
To My left. There is a pig race. There is the race of pigs. Avoid.
The crowd stokes nausea and stirs contempt.
Someone left a mass of hair on the street.
A choleric baby screams in its caboose, its face pinkened with anger spots. Babies scream because they are manipulative.
I look at the sky. The sky's taint is a melancholic yellow.
I am trapped in a glassy geranium. Diaphanous walls surround Me. I am within an unwitnessed enclosure. Instead of receding, the horizon tightens slowly.
Befreckled girls order plumes of cotton candy.

I approach a booth the sign of which reads:
"FONDLE FOR A BUCK."

A candy-eyed filly offers her lips to the passers-by. Engarlanded around her neck is a necklace of skin.
A tri-legged old man is hungry for a slobber. His right leg tapers to a stub. His mouth bare; he shows a dentured grimace. He grabs her cheeks and pushes his nose into her face. Gripped with revulsion, she slowly tenders her mouth. He shapes and simonizes her breast-bulbs, as if he wanted them to infuse him with their florescent youth.
Does he want to suffuse her body with age?
She is dazed by the soporific heat. Her white shirt inspires him with a new vigor. He sticks his hands into the arm-holes of her sleeveless shirt. He models her heat-blistered arms with his heavy, old hands. He descends to her thighs, hoists her checkerboard skirt, and licks the flaps of her hips.
He palms the mobile garden of her pubic area.

Besotted and longing for My attention, Gabriela walks slowly through the curtain and stands before Me, holding a piece of paper in her quavering hands.

She reads:

"Long after the great wars, the sun shuddered to a quiescent gray, the birds consumed their young, the dandelions withered, and a man was born from the haunches of a cat.

"The man found himself anonymous and, because of his anonymity, embarked upon an ill-defined search to discover his name.

"For one hundred days, he walked through the infinite expanse of a beachscape, moving along in a senseless odyssey.

"The liquid sun rose.

"The man came upon a meager grove which sustained itself on the sandy ground.

"Reaching out his hand to grasp an orange from its native tree, the man found the fruit, upon its seizure, glutted and sodden with larvae.

"Disgusted, the man cast it down to the sand.

"A jackdaw lighted from a sulphurous cloud onto the tree, which was nearly blackened to a crisp.

"Deadened with malaise, the weary man drudged on.

"He wore thick, opaque goggles over his squinting eyes, a poultice for the sun's sear.

"He was garbed in a tunic woven from the wings of butterflies and human scalps.

"He envisioned a figure on the sand, hunched-over and inert.

"When the man addressed the stranger, he declared that he was on a pilgrimage through the fringelands.

"His goal was to reach the forbidden regions.

"The man said, 'I will accompany you. I have been walking on this beach for four hundred years or perhaps it has been only one day. My life may be nearing its conclusion, and I would also like to know what lies in the zone of the damned.'

"They waited until the morning sang its crystalline dirge.

"The next morning, the two men bound themselves together with a strand of kelp-dross that had washed up with the morning tide.

"They walked, and as they walked, their footfalls vanished as soon as they were formed.

"They saw many wonders: headless hippopotami, animated vegetables the size of pyramids, cluttered mounds of skeletons, and disconnected fleshless bone.

"Yet the most astonishing of all of these unheard-of sights was a gigantic tower of glass, a labyrinthine structure in which windows bled into windows in eternal configurations.

"'The missionaries live in that tower,' said the stranger, pointing.

"'I need a revolver,' his companion exclaimed anxiously.

"He was fearful, for he had often heard of the purging of the land, the unspeakable horrors that were the works of the missionaries' surgical hands.

"The stranger said slowly, shaking his head in disagreement, 'A revolver will not cease the attack of a missionary. They can be bribed, however.'

"'With what?' questioned the journeyman.

"'With a human nose' was the response.

"'It is better to lose a nose than to be imprisoned in the torture chambers of the missionaries.'

"They dressed in the hides of oxen carcasses.

"Masqueraded, they ventured across a wide gorge.

"At the summit of the gorge was a mahogany door.

"No building was attached to the door.

"It was a portal that stood solitarily amid the endless landscape of sand dunes.

"On the door was a single word.

"That word was HUMANITY.

"Inexplicably, the stranger fell into a deep swoon and collapsed onto the hardened sandy ground.

"And he slept.

"For days, he slept.

"His sleep was shattered by a shuffling sound and a muted screech.

"The voyager slipped out of the door, shrilling madly.

Joseph Suglia

"His eyes were canceled out.

"From his eye-pores trickled a clear, colorless fluid.

"His mouth disgorged globules of blood as he tumbled down, spasming violently.

"The stranger approached the writhing body of the voyager, questioning him hysterically: 'WHAT DID YOU SEE? WHAT DID YOU SEE?'

"'Lobotomize the children,' the dying man intoned in a whisper. 'Lobotomize the children.'

"His breath stilled in the untethered breeze, his twisted body sightlessly envisioning the oncoming waves."

The sharp-pecking thrushes dance in the furrows of the rocks.

A beer bottle bursts open.

Hyperbubbling beermilk blasts out of the shattered beer bottle.

Watch out for the shattered fragments of glass.

Each fragment is an impaler.

A shard of glass plunges into My liquid flesh.

A tangle of skin-syrup twists on its gaping point.

The glass penetrates My interior.

The beer emulsifies and froths. Emulsions of beer splatter onto My forehead.

I hear the sounds of stealthy animals rustling in the leaves. A mellow race of fringe-creatures amasses and mingles.

Within My body are herds of angry animals.

Vermicular forms sinuate into My anus. They tremble in their wormy orgy, tearing at My small intestine with microscopic bites.

A pellucid membrane envelops Me. I am caught in the transparent sac of flesh. I am trapped in the sac like a petal in a vermin's hot mouth.

I tear open the invisible skin without effort. I rise from the sticky amnion.

The breath of midnight massages My face.

126

Grasshoppers rasp, clinging to their orange peel lunch. They greedily devour the orange peel in an orgy of clicking warbles. A wasp lands on a corpse-skin curtain; its pellucid hair-thin wings flap frenziedly.

Cabbages flutter in My ears like voracious ear mites.

I splash through puddles of placental sludge and amniotic fluid.

My eyes are beginning to deglaciate.

My eyes, they burgeon forth.

Curtains of champagne light envelop Me. At the core of the light is a darkness. A black void stares at Me with diabolical intent.

The night-insects beckon Me to enter the black abyss.

My skin is deliquescent.

I enter the glowing penumbra.

The yew trees are forever weeping strange fluids. The fluids are many-colored. Tears of mucous drip down their emaciated branches.

My skeleton begins to warp.

I wade through the sludge. The slush gushes inward, forming a vortical spiral.

My skin resembles the glistening skin of a jellyfish. My anal orifice resembles the corolla of a flower.

The squillae bury themselves in the mud.

The waves uncoil and unebb.

I am an unraveling ribbon of liquid.

A frothy lather covers Me.

Along the shore of the beach glisten spiralline coils of shark rejectamenta.

The carnivorous seaworms dance for My amusement.

The sea urchins are mired in the putrific ooze.

From the branches of the yew trees are forever dripping icicles of oceanic gelatin.

In front of Me is a sea-cube, undulating nautical pudding. A translucent pillar of sea-liquid. The column wobbles. The water, it is turquoise. The water is solid, a thick viscous mass.

Sap slushes down the bark of the yew tree.

The sap resembles salmon residuum.

Joseph Suglia

My mind is a prison.

Dead fetuses climb out of necro-wombs of eternal silence.

The parasoled women spill and mill out of the Crystalline Hotel. One of the women slowly approaches Me. Her face is lost in a nightmare-black mane. Her hair grows and grows until it becomes a manta.

Her hair becomes the universe. Expanding and voracious, it devours space.

The woman is triple-eyed. Three yellow discs of feline oglers.

Her eye-discs stare at Me.

A strobe light sparkles with artificial coruscation. Spangles of light shatter into frost and light-spume.

A deer arches into a madding run. It is swallowed by a penumbra. Its silhouette absents itself from the sleeping day.

I weave My way through a dense canopy of herbage. I climb over a sewer pipe entangled in snarls of vines. I enter a grassy depression. The tall halms wriggle. I careen through the steep grass and over the rain-pelted moss.

On the wet ground is a matted cat-corpse. Globs of brain matter sinuate through skull-punctures.

I want to slice the cat open ever-so slowly and garb My body with its inner totems. Lunging and clawing, I tear into its belly and fondle its soft intestines. I grope its viscera, its gristle and yellowish gut, the meaty mother-of-pearl sap, the bedraggled cords of intestinal tubing. I rip out the cat's intestines in strands and threads.

I invade the cat's larynx and plunge into her palpitating viscera. I nuzzle the cat's insides. Gliding through her pulsating network of slime-lubricated tubes, I swirl into black deadness. I burst into the honeycombs of her intestines. I worm through gunk-slimed tubes. I squirm into the pores of her skin. I tear My blood-smeared face from the cat hide and sigh with dark pleasure.

The cat is not dead.

The cat licks My cheek with her folded tongue in an act of insane worship.

Her eye is splintered into oozing halves, each of which emits a whitish discharge.

128

The fluid of the night cascades through the sky.

Watch out.

The night, it is phosphorescent.
I am the soul-unspooling memory of the night.
The women sway into the grove.
The aqueous bladder of the night is unseamed.
The pink windmills spiral madly.
The night's thick protoplasm spreads over everything.
Everything I do, everything that I have ever done, is a preparation for death.
I am fascinated by the reverse heliotropism of nightflowers.
My body softens. It is dissipating into the night.
The sky is asmear with hyalescent corn juice.
I see the unseaming of the morn's aqueous bladder.
This nocturnal sojourn draws Me deep into the most obscure recesses of the night.
This nightscape will soon be burnt alive by the sadistic light.
I halt My twirling ballet. I am pinioned in a vast, lightless space. I am transfixed in the void.
Rancid vegetables spiral in the milky clouds sublime maggot-devoured turnips swirling into a vortex verdigris-encrusted metallic refuse everywhere the felicity of slime.
The spotlight fizzles. Where are the willowy women?
The women are, in fact, not women. They are whitish female mannequins smeared with black paint. The black paint spreads over their stretching finger-webs.
From the branches of the yew tree dangles a gibbet.
The gibbet seems to grin.
I am waiting for a signature to cross these fathomless skies.
I am waiting for an emblem.
What does all of this mean?
What does it mean?
I approach the Crystalline Hotel.

Watch out.

A band of angry baboons encircles the hotel, starving with the desire for electric skin.

Entry

Monday darkens into evening. I haven't yet checked out of the Crystalline Hotel. I have no idea what to do with Myself. A telephone call from Dr. Mendoza seems unlikely.

I sidle down the corridors of the hotel until I reach the exit. I veil My eyes from the glare of the declining sun, My wrist leaning firmly against My corrugated brow.

I glide down Impression Avenue.

On the pavement is a gored plum. Black beetles swarm over its skin.

A salivating mutt bends lightly over the plum and licks it.

I cross an endless parking lot.

There is very little vegetation in Benton Harbor. Ten years ago, most of the natural yew trees in Benton Harbor were uprooted and replaced with artificial yew trees. I like artificial trees better, anyhow.

A blue-suited pamphleteer shouts into a megaphone. His grainy hair, partly saturated with shoe polish, fans in the evening breeze. He fulminates at an unseen crowd.

"Our lives are evanescent. Beauty comes and goes. There is nothing to hold onto. You have a wife. She is beautiful. But then her beauty is no more. Gone."

His mandibles flop up and down.

"We are but lacy ephemerae circling in the air. There is more to life than life and death. There is a place beyond this world."

The skin on his face is galvanized with spiderlike electric currents.

A spectral energy surfaces to his cheeks, causing them to give off a penumbral glow.

As I approach him, My shadow shrouds his face. He sees Me.

"You there, what comes after death?"

Speaking to Me.

"You, sir, what comes after death?"

"What comes after death?"

He nods energetically.

Traversing the lot, I say to the back of his auburn head,

"Decomposition."

The man in the crowd desires Me intensely. He is exiled from the country of My desire. He tries to escape from his solitude by desiring Me. He desires Me in order to strengthen his feeling of power.

His desire intensifies and rises to love.

What is love?

Love is the desire for control.

And yet the more he loves, the more the lover's power shrinks and withers.

Love is the darkest of all emotions.

Love brings out the worst in people.

Love has nothing to do with ethics.

He who loves, loves in order to have a thing to love. The person whom he loves becomes like a prosthetic appendage, an organ without which he cannot live. The lover cannot function outside of his beloved's space of activity. When he loves, love suffuses the lover's entire being. Its force is felt in every filament. Love throws him into his deeper dimensions. The person whom he loves is free from his love and therefore causes him the

greatest agitation. He grows enraged because the one whom he loves disdains to requite that love. In his rage, he strives to murder the one he loves, precisely because the beloved is absolutely free from his love. He wants to consume him, make him a part of himself, turn him into a mute object.
The crowd is love.

I will find Dr. Mendoza and have My interview. The fact that I haven't received a telephone call from him is profoundly insulting. That dirty fucker denied Me My interview. Dr. Mendoza invited Me to the Benton Harbor Community College to be interviewed for a tenure-stream position. I received an e-mail from him in which he stated this explicitly.

And Miss Grimmlager? Her ignorance was studied. She knew exactly who I am. She sent Me three e-mail messages. She made it quite clear in the last of them that an emissary from the community college would retrieve Me at the station. On the day on which My interview was scheduled, the emissary did not appear.

Secretaries, like dogs, are all fascists.

No one ever forgets Jonathan Barrows.

I did not receive the interview that I was promised. That is blasphemy. I do not wish to teach at this asylum of an institution. Nonethehowever, I demand an interview. Dr. Mendoza will interview Me, or I will kill him.

Either/or.

Simply because murder is "illegal," this does not mean that it is "immoral." What is allowed by the state has nothing to do with questions of right and wrong. What is right or wrong is determined by Me. Whatever pleases Me is right. That which does not please Me is

wrong. I do whatever pleases Me, and, if it pleases Me to kill, then I will kill.

Watch out.

If Dr. Mendoza distinguished himself at all in the scholarly realm, it was only by virtue of his intransigently rebellious spirit. When it was published thirty-two years ago, Mendoza's only book, *The Pornographic Classroom* was deemed scandalous by some and regarded with smirking amusement by most others. A self-published work that outlines a "new" pedagogy, it is marked by an almost complete disregard for classical educational theory; indeed, it dispenses with documentation in any form.

The book's premise is as follows: Educational institutions have created unnecessary barriers between teachers and students or "subjects," as Mendoza calls them. The author maintains that the instructional relationship is superimposed upon the erotic relationship. The time is propitious, Mendoza argues, to initiate an intense intimacy between instructors and "subjects."

Instructors, according to Mendoza, should copulate with their students on an ever-expanding basis. The classroom experience, Mendoza proposes, should return to its frenzied provenance, which he calls "erogenous knowledge."

The departments to which Mendoza applied for tenure-stream positions considered *The Pornographic Classroom* to be the fruit of a crackpot's lucubrations. By following his more wayward impulses, Dr. Mendoza had dug himself into a steep career grave.

Much like Myself, Dr. Mendoza was expelled from scholarly communities and could only secure an

academic position in the School of Learning at the Benton Harbor Community College, where scholarly prestige is of negligible importance.

Despite his disesteemed reputation, Dr. Mendoza quickly made a name for himself in Benton Harbor as a sexological guru. A spellbinding lecturer, he held his classroom audiences in thrall. The administration, at first, implored Dr. Mendoza to place in check his unorthodox views; when the course evaluations were returned, however, the Dean of Studies recognized that this was a man of enormous drawing power.

Dr. Mendoza lectures to this day on the essence of human relationships to legions of rapt spectators. He has taught at the Benton Harbor Community College for thirty years.

If Dr. Mendoza refuses to interview Me, I will kill him. Cut him open, and watch him bleed. If he offers Me a position, I will bite off his nose and spit it back in his face.

A glob of blood will form on his face.
When the world gets in My way, I devour it.

No matter what happens, I am going to pound him with My fists. I will bloody his nose and break his teeth.

I saunter stealthily through the filthy corridors of the community college, My blood simmering, with revenge on My mind.

No one denies Jonathan Barrows an interview.

I reach room 121.

It is here that Dr. Mendoza will instruct the seminar. In thirty-five minutes.

I AM GOING TO GET HIM.

The classroom is unentered. Within are twenty chairs, a slightly egg-smeared blackboard (*shreds of eggy putrescence litter the podium*), an overhead projector, a professorial desk with a lectern, and a professorial closet.

A Hyundai coasts into the parking lot of the Benton Harbor Community College.

I open the door of the professorial closet and look inside. Within are stubby bits of chalk, a plunger, and random blue test booklets.

I climb into the narrow space. I leave the door open slightly. From within the confines of the professorial closet, I will spy upon Dr. Mendoza.

When the appropriate time comes, I will leap forward and demand My interview. If he refuses to grant Me My interview, I will annihilate him. Even if he does grant Me an interview, I will pummel him with My fists.

I will break him open.

The automobile gears into an unmarked parking space.

I wait impatiently.

For My entire life, I have been disinherited, disfranchised, and dishonored. I have been denied what rightfully belongs to Me. My property has been expropriated.

They've thrown Me from My throne in order to still their pain.

I am the exciter of all passions — in particular, the passion of envy. For this reason, My former "advisor"

136

slandered Me. I can't even get an interview at Benton Harbor Community College.

But does it matter, ultimately? Why become a priest of knowledge?

There is no such thing as knowledge.

Everything that we think we know is false.

Indeed, we know absolutely nothing.

Our ideas do not correspond with the way that things actually are.

Everything that we have been taught is a lie.

We are not who we think we are.

The world is not what we imagine it to be.

Everyone you think you know is a stranger.

You are even a stranger to yourself.

I am absolutely unknowable to you.

All of our thoughts are mismatched with the world.

We live our lives steeped in ignorance.

I wait in the professorial closet.

I am waiting for Dr. Mendoza to teach Me.

I wait to be educated.

My Eyes Have Seen the Coming of the Glory of the Lord

Into the classroom they solemnly parade, the night students.

I recognize the waiter from Ye Olde Diner. There is the hotel clerk. There is Miss Grimmlager. There is Gabriela. There is Manuela. There is the old pigfucker. There are Sushi and Butterworth. *Why are they still in Benton Harbor?* There is the German woman. There is the young man.

That must be Dr. Mendoza. Who else could it be? Dr. Mendoza would resemble David Bowie, if David Bowie were wiglessly bald and weighed three hundred pounds.

His mouth quivers and emits a dull groan that bears a distinct resemblance to the cry of a lactating musk ox.

I am disgusted by the drooping folds of his obesity.

I am resolved to have My interview.

And yet what is this strange feeling of hesitation that surfaces inside of Me?

I must flee this satanic banquet.

And yet I cannot. I cannot stay, and yet I cannot leave. I cannot look, but I cannot avert My eyes.

Watch out.

Dr. Mendoza's leather-gloved fingers slide along the midriff of a slender cigarette. He pinches the cigarette between the middle finger and the thumb of his right hand and gently strokes the shaft. He lifts his bowlike arms in supplication and parts his lips to speak. I

Joseph Suglia

retract into the shadows and listen. His eyes glistening with fervor, Dr. Mendoza addresses the classroom.

"Do you not hear the cry of the planet? It is summoning you to enter the community. How do you respond to this call? How do you become part of the community? The answer is simple: Marry!"

Manuela breathes a sigh of recognition.

Dr. Mendoza's pearly eyes wink knowingly.

"Marriage is not, as is often thought, a simple thing. It is not merely the union of two self-contained individuals. When she marries, a lady is no longer an individual. She is now a member of the community. A gentleman, when he marries, is no longer an individual. He, too, is now a member of the community. They are not merely bound to one another. Together, they are bound to the community. Together, they have family fun."

His forehead furrows.

"Marriage seals your contract with the commonweal; it stamps your individuality with a *social* character. Before, you were a bohemian dressed in a black turtleneck, chewing on a licorice stick in your dismal single-cell apartment. Now, for the first time, you are a fully functioning human being. We, the members of this great human congregation, welcome you! You now belong to our venerable guild!"

Dr. Mendoza waves his right index finger at the class as if he were prohibiting a band of shepherds from having sexual congress with the animals on his farm.

He declares in a stentorian voice, "A woman is not woman unless she is married to a man. A man is not a man unless he is married to a woman.

"Once you become married, you will produce children who will, someday, also become part of this

140

vast human ocean which is the community. That is how you give back what the community has given you! Your children — those endlessly yelping domestic beasts — will, someday, grow up and marry themselves! This is how the community perpetuates itself.

"One must not think of marriage, then, as a personal relationship. I do not fuck my wife's vagina. The community fucks her vagina. My wife's vagina is not my personal property. Her vagina belongs to the community."

His peppered eyebrows join hands.

"The pleasures of life are not restricted to those of the solitaire. Nothing is more joyous than a wedding, and no one is happier than a spouse! Oh the sweet joys of communal being-together! Give up your solitude, and be part of this great human mosaic which is life!

"All of this whoop-de-do about the individual! An 'individual' is nothing more than someone who ignores his social destination; as a result, he will never be something greater than himself. His life will never be socially productive — and thus will never be meaningful. The anti-conjugals should realize that they are, in fact, not 'rebels' at all. They refuse to marry. But by doing so, they are still playing by the community's rules. It is pointless to refuse to be usual. The more you dissent, the more you affirm the system. There is a place in the system for those who resist the system."

My fingers shudder in a riot of manic clattering.

"The cult of the individual teaches that every person is singular. I can scarcely agree. If each is unlike the other, what should we say of twins? I have a cousin who is a twin. Her names are Shelly and Deborah. She

is two and yet simultaneously one. Twins baffle any notion of personal uniqueness.

"The individualists think of themselves as isolated atoms floating through space. But even their very physical makeup belies this assumption. What sense is there to speak of an individualized nervous system? There is but one nervous system that we all hold in common. We are all glued together in an invisible web, that myriadic network which we call 'life'! If I smash my fist on the table — like so! (*He brings his fist down upon the professorial table, which rattles as he strikes it*) — someone in Czechoslovakia is bound to feel the reverberation."

Dr. Mendoza enunciates clearly, sternly stretching out his words. His mind is an empty Ziploc bag.

"Shatter your sanctuaries! Burn down your citadels! Raze them to the ground! Tear down the screens that shield you from other human beings!"

Dr. Mendoza pauses and addresses the desk clerk, "Through the windy window, I have seen your slender, youthful body conversing with other young men.

"Give yourselves up! Give yourselves up to the community! Only your self-surrender will insure your immortality."

Dr. Mendoza salutes the class with a firm, upraised arm.

Enough!

I spring out of the professorial closet and wave My hands with indignation.

Watch out.

I shout at Dr. Mendoza's incredulous face, "What NONSENSE! There is no pleasure in marriage!

Marriage is purely functional and has nothing to do with enjoyment!"

Dr. Mendoza sputters and splutters.

The students do not respond. It is as if they were expecting Me.

"When you get married, a contract binds you to another individual. A certificate, a license, an 'official' document authorizes your union. You are joined together by the state, and your relationship is now the property of the state. What was once a personal relationship has become a mechanical relationship.

"A married couple resembles two animals chained together. Now that you're married, you can't get away from your wife, no matter how much she may revolt you. Both of you are *forced* to love each other — no matter how disastrous your union may be. Your wife insults you, takes up your space, robs you of sleep, pilfers your money, borrows your possessions without your permission — and you're *obligated by law* to stay with her. She disgusts you. She eats her yogurt sloppily. She is a bloated mass of tissue. She has poor hygiene, blabbers, slobbers, and froths — and still you can't disengage yourself from her. The law manacles you together.

"A spouse is a tapeworm in your gut, a parasite that has attached itself to your body.

"You're no longer with your wife because you desire her flesh. You're no longer with her for your own self-amusement. You're with her because you have no other choice. A bond binds both of you together. To sunder that bond would be a violation of the law.

"Say what you will, but marriage *does* destroy solitude — and without solitude, there is no longer the possibility of becoming someone else. One who has

lost the possibility of becoming someone else is a corpse.

"Life is the ever-generating, infinitely multiplying source of possibilities. Once you become married, you destroy all possibilities exclusive of being-married. You are 'off the market,' so to speak, much like a sausage purchased at a butcher's shop.

"A spouse is a dead man. Married couples are drained of their vitality. Inevitably, you and your wife grow old in your hatred of each other. You hate your wife because you see her as a vile sapper of possibilities."

Marriage handcuffs the hands of possibility.
— Jonathan Barrows

"Because marriage restricts possibility, it must be condemned.

"How DARE you, sir, question the supremacy of the individual! The individual is the origin of all value, not the community! It is the extraordinary individual who determines what is meaningful. He alone brings things of value into the world. If for no other reason, this is why the individual comes before the community.

"The community is only meaningful insofar as it relates to Me. This is My community! *The community is My property. I can do with it what I please!* I have no desire to hold anyone's hand and sing.

"You communitarians! You worship the throng. You idolize the average. Someday, even the sewers will be crowded. In this culture, everything is reduced to the ordinary. Everyone is forced to be the same as everyone else. Everything that is said repeats what one already knows. Nothing must remain extraordinary.

Nothing must remain mysterious. What we are witnessing is *the banalization of the world.*

"Nowhere is this more evident than at this 'place of learning.' What you teach is merely the reaffirmation of what students already believe. This excremental institution DOESN'T EVEN DESERVE TO BE CALLED A 'COLLEGE'! Never have I seen such a pack of morons in My life!

"ALL OF YOU ARE POOR! ALL OF YOU ARE STUPID! AND BECAUSE YOU ARE POOR AND STUPID, YOU ARE RELIGIOUS FANATICS, AS WELL! AND WORST OF ALL ... YOU ARE THE SLAVES OF THE STATE!"

Before Me is an army of aged students. Their mouths grotesquely disfigured into grimaces, they laugh humorlessly.

Radiating malice, their eyes study Me intensely.

Their wormlike tongues beat their lower lips, flagellating the lust-heavy air.

They advance upon Me, starving, angry, desperate.

I am trapped within this solemn space.

Manuela stands up quiveringly and glares at Me with a thick mixture of lust and loathing. Her eyes glowering diabolically, she says to My mind, "You think you're so good. You think you're so good, Mister Mincemeat. You're not so good. We're gonna show you that you're just like us."

Suddenly, a bare arm bursts forth and clenches My wrist with savage intensity. Butterworth and Sushi bite My arm, which sends a shock through My body, paralyzing Me.

Sharp blows shoot through My veins. Manuela grapples Me close as I fight for resistance. She tears off the sleeve of My monogrammed shirt in a burst of fury, wrenching free the flimsy fabric. She hoists her black skirt and rips off her panties; I see an ocean of floating wriggling pink between her legs, the hollow vaginal mouth. She flays My shirt; I stand there bare-chested. Butterworth and Sushi drive Me down to the ground.

As they hold My arms down, Manuela presses her flapping buttocks against My nose and rubs them against My full, generous lips. I lose Myself in her restless anal hair. I smell the stench of greasy faeces and the damp reek of urine.

While Butterworth and Sushi's arms are locked around My own, Manuela's mouth devours My shoulders. Skinned and dangling like a helpless marionette, I am loose and mangled in her overpowering grip, a metallic claw.

My head falls back into the night sky as she rapaciously bites My chest. My bitten and fingernail-scratched shoulders become one with the void that swallows Me. Manuela nuzzles, fawning, My naked rib cage.

The classroom crew awakens from their sleep of death. They, the mob, fall onto Me with truculent hands. Pawing and lunging, they consume My wriggling body.

I squirm within a prison of arms and legs, inextricably tangled in a web of joints and fingers.

The darkness is torn down in streamers.

The mob is a fleshy octopus. Its tentacles shoot out in all directions and grapple Me.

The young man seizes My neck in a choke hold. The waiter crouches onto My legs, which now seem frail, and presses My elbows bleeding into the ground. He slaps My face agonistically and wrenches My flesh.

The dirty waiter asks Me, "YOU THINK YOU'RE SO GOOD, DON'T YOU? YOU THINK YOU'RE SO GOOD?"

For a moment, I free Myself from his clawing hands. I push him back. His polyp-like body spills across the floor. I vault toward the door, making bounds through the air. *She unabashedly stared at My penis as she tore open her blouse.*

Eddies of naked bodies surround Me. They straightjacket My arms, shackling them behind My back, seizing them tightly, firming their grip.

A volley of shocks jackhammer against My arms and back. Pain floods My senses; I can hear the sound of granulating bone.

It is as if they were slicing My flesh in sections, pulling out My innards with gloved hands.

Dr. Mendoza violently undoes his trousers and lunges at My neck. Twisting My right arm behind My back, the desk clerk thrashes My neck with his tongue. Someone sticks a pudendal tongue into the glyphic arabesques of My ear. The clavicle of My ear-cartilage is moistened by its wine-dark touch. Dr. Mendoza motions semaphorically to the others with a freed palm.

"Come, students! Come here!"

The rabid horde of aging schoolchildren complies. I am spread-eagled onto the blindingly white wall, My arms stretched out and pinned on each side. They stroke and kiss My throat. I am chained by the coiling appendages of the writhing fleshy octopus. Their tentacular arms bind Me on all sides.

The desk clerk undoes My belt and strips down My trousers and J.B. boxer briefs.

Watch out.

Gabriela cradles My smooth leg, sliding down its length like a firefighter. She tenderly suckles the bud of My kneecap. The German woman lashes out and grips My penis, which she proceeds to stroke and strike ferociously. Her caress transports shocks through My veins. Her hands are spasmodic.

Dr. Mendoza commands, "Open the window! I need air!"

The waiter uncloses the window.

The thrashing fetus of a robin lies in its nest on the window sill.

Its embryonic mandarin talons are pulverizable and frail; its wizened flesh squirms in frenzied bursts.

Gurgles of laughter. The aerie spills over the ledge, spirals downward, and splatters noiselessly below.

They, the mob, screech their war cry and cluster into a stampede of rabid, starved cattle, frothing psychopaths with skin-hungry mouths.

They cover Me with sinister embraces, driving Me back down to the floorboards. Wriggling and wiggling, I stand up again.

Their hands grope for My appendages — an arm or a leg — as if I were the main course in a seafood banquet.

The desk clerk manacles one of My fluttering legs. Their faces are nightmarishly contorted into black daemon masks. The mob is famished for My flesh.

Foreign fingers invade the corolla of My anal orifice.

I am surrounded by rank hagiophiliacs with sodden, sagging, withered, pendulous breasts.

I am surrounded by rank hagiophiliacs with dangling, serpentine penises.

I stand up again with superhuman effort.

Butterworth launches forward, grasps My hair, and pummels Me savagely to the uncarpeted floor, pinning Me down with both arms. Hands and legs fetter My hands and legs. I shove her off.

The desk clerk cranes out his neck and bites My bared shoulder. I start in pain and freeze. I scramble to regain My balance, but the desk clerk and the old man hold Me fast. I lie prostrate on the ground.

There are too many of them. Limp, pliable bodies swarm over Me like man-sized maggots. I struggle to regain My balance, while pushing off the fawning, nuzzling, grasping bodies.

Dr. Mendoza stands on the professorial desk and desk-dives onto My shoulders, driving Me back down to the ground. He clutches My neck ferociously. Pawing and fondling, he weighs Me down with his immense bulk. A squirming heap of unclad bodies accumulate on My back. My body, it is trampled, steamrolled under falling, salacious torsos. They drive Me down, down, further down.

Their vague mouths spread open impossibly, widening into skies. Their mouths mouth Me; they kiss and suck. I hear an electric fizzle.

A buzzing, white-hot shock machine firms its grip on My skull, crushing My mind into a cerebral mash.

Sushi places her face in the cleft between My buttocks and sticks her tongue deep into My rectum. She probes My anal orifice, lapping and licking it like a dog. I feel her groping, webbed fingers inside of Me.

Miss Grimmlager defecates and ingests her faeces. A clownish grin widens on her misshapen face.

Butterworth and Sushi tear off each other's clothing.

Sushi buries her face into the streaming, undone garments of her counterpart. An unclothed Sushi protrudes a heliotropic tongue and probes and laps Butterworth's ear.

Dr. Mendoza sucks My widening anus, prodding and stretching it open with his fingers.

A shadowy mouth expectorates into My eyes. The glob of saliva resembles lactate.

Midgets with stiletto blades slicing up the bull-ox, you fill My mouth with pain.

Manuela shouts imperatively, "Get the plunger! Get the plunger!"

Her face caked with greasy faeces, Miss Grimmlager rummages through the professorial closet. Dr. Mendoza seizes My penis and grabs My testicles. He shakes My penis vigorously.

They are like bloodsucking old men nesting around a pink fresh babe, their teeth ready to descend.

My arms are raised like a weathervane angel.

I cringe and agonize, curl and wither. Foreign hands blast My penis. Their vulgar fingers slope into stalactites, throbbing fleshy pulsers.

As poised as a cobra, Miss Grimmlager stands and lifts the plunger. She tosses it gracefully to Dr. Mendoza. Dr. Mendoza, in turn, boomerangs the plunger to Manuela, who catches it and raises it into the air triumphantly.

Manuela shouts her cry of victory, "I GOT IT! I GOT THE PLUNGER!"

With elder's privilege ringing in his voice, the old man barks, "TURN HIM ON HIS CHEST!"

Now supine, I look up in horror. Manuela advances upon Me, brandishing the plunger.

My head slams against the ground.

She pushes the suction cup of the device firmly against My buttocks.

My flesh-stumps pound the floor.

My cadaver bedraggled with blood, I will die with the tale unspoken on My scar-wrinkled lips.

Hammering wildly, Manuela plunges the funnel of My anus, as if she wanted to draw out the contents of My lower intestine.

She intones darkly, *"Satan —*

"Satan is sodomizing you —

"Satan is an anal rapist."

Spent, I attempt to stand and then collapse lifelessly on the floor of the classroom, My tongue lolling uselessly out of My mouth. A chair is raised and smashes down on My skull, deadening My consciousness.

I precipitate into the abyss, swirling downwards into the ever-present black.

The hands fall on Me.

The world blacks out.

When I revive, I see Dr. Mendoza lecturing to the eyes that stare at My exhausted body, "Never before have I witnessed such a downfall ... What delusions of grandeur ... Let this be a learning experience ..."

I huddle on the floor of the classroom. My tear-stricken head rocks in clawing hands. My teeth glued together, I plead to unheeding cacodaemons.

I am as damaged as a tomato on a schooner helmed by shanty-chanting sailors.

I weep, wrenched, doubled-over; I grasp My hair; furiously, I writhe. I spread open My embrittled fingers. My welted hands are loose-fitting gloves dangling electrically in space.

I sink.

The spasms subside and then stir again. I can see the early dawn stars of the early dawn.

Dr. Mendoza drains a pitcher of water into the crevasses of My face.

The element rushes freezing into My eyes. The emptied decanter clatters to the wooden planks.

Forgive Me, God, for My blasphemy.

I look down and see the viscous moistness. A glistening, mucid substance coats My fingertips. The violent motions of their hands brought Me to a mechanical ejaculation.

Tears stream hotly down My face.

Until now, My interior was divinely unpenetrated. I remained intact and clean.

They slimed their bodies inside of My own. They encroached upon My pristine interior. They invaded My solitude, infringing upon what was unbesmirched. They soiled Me. They broke into My silent citadel. They held down My flapping legs and penetrated Me. My legs fluttered and fanned.

I am polluted by their filth.

I am contaminated by the shit of the world.

My cell is made permeable to the outside.

Without My permission, they manipulated My body, using it as if it were a toy or an instrument.

Before, I lorded over the world. The world was My property.

Now I am deposed.
My consciousness is breaking apart.

Manuela looks at My face with a slight measure of pity and says, "There's no sense in crying over spilt semen."

Now I know.
Now I understand.
Now I understand why these things happened.
Now I understand why these things happened to Me.
Now I understand why that which is happening to Me is happening to Me.
Now I know why these things are happening to Me.
Desire is hatred.
Desire is hatred.
Desire is hatred.
Desire is hatred.
Desire is hatred.
Desire is hatred.

Midnight Ebony

The night flows through the window now.
The enclosing night.
I am alone in this benighted space.
I disappear into the seams of the protective night.
The writhing black welcomes me lovingly.
It is impossible for me to move.
At this moment, I know, like never before, the destitution of the world.
I am the destitution of the world.
My violation is the outcome of a theorem. It is a theorem of desire.
To be universally desired is to be universally hated.
He who is universally desired is universally hated.
I am universally desired and therefore universally hated.
Q.E.D.
All of Benton Harbor is a landscape of shadows.
A crackling comes from the ceiling.
Look upward. The ceiling is rupturing.
A gaping void opens up, a pit ripping open the fabric of space. Shapes germinate from the hole in the ceiling.
Black psuedopods dangle out of the hole, waving tentacles reaching for me. The tentacles thrash violently.
A shock of pain shoots through my brain. What's that?
Damn fucking hornet.
No, it's a butterfly.
An ebony butterfly.
A big black motherfucking butterfly.
Watch out.
Butterflies don't sting. Do they? But my skin's been perforated. The winged thing bit me.

Joseph Suglia

More beast than insect, the massive creature hovers over me, extending its black plumage, its wings beating madly. Its maw opens and closes, dripping gobs of mucilage onto my forehead.

The mouth of the butterfly pullulates translucent gelatin. The viscous goo gets into my eyes, making them glossy and useless.

Its suppurating mouth resembles a beak.

My face broadens in alarm.

The fervent flapping of the butterfly's wings resounds in my ears.

In a mad spasm of clicking and fluttering, the butterfly levitates near my left ear as if it wanted to fly into its canal. Its colorless plumage shatters into shards of black icicles that tear apart the silken film of the night.

Suspended in the nocturnal air, the black butterfly seethes.

Nothing is more terrifying than the presence of a butterfly.

II

Walking with a Switchblade in Hand through Streets of Pain

At the age of twenty-eight, I murdered My so-called "dissertation advisor."

Simply because murder is *illegal*, this does not imply that it is *unethical*. Whatever is *ethical* pleases Me. Whatever is unethical does not please Me. Based on this definition, if it pleases Me to kill, then killing is My right.[1]

He destroyed My career.

In his letter of condemnation, My "advisor" wrote: "Mr. Barrows is far too serious to be taken seriously as a scholar."

On more than one occasion, he took Me by the shoulders and shook Me fiercely, shouting, *"Good God, man, get out of the library and swim in the deep currents of life! Real life isn't in the books!"*

Whenever someone says, "Get out of the library!" that person means, "I want you to be as illiterate as I am."

Whenever someone calls you a "nerd," that person means, "Your powers of thought exceed My own."

A "nerd" is someone who is smarter than you.

[1] Ethics is not based on God, some supersensible truth, or what a culture determines as its "morality." Ethics is based on the self, its agonies and its pleasures. Each individual has his or her own *ethics*. What is ethical for Me may not be ethical for you, and vice versa. Although you may consider killing an absolute wrong, I may consider it an absolute right. No one can legislate in the name of ethics except for the absolute self. My interpretation of the ethics of murder passes close to that of Max Stirner, *Der Einzige und sein Eigenthum.*

Joseph Suglia

I had the Career Development Office send his *Verdammungsbrief* to a female professor in the Department of Philosophy who wanted Me to insert My penis into her vaginal cavity.

She e-mailed Me, "Johnny, darling, please stop by as quickly as you can."

The office was heavy with thought. She handed Me the piece of paper. Nothing about the letter surprised Me.

I had forever reached the point where his feelings, his ideas, did not matter to Me. His seething irritation, his malicious whisperings, met with indifference. I did not curry his favor; I did not seek his attention; I had no desire to impress him.

I saw him as he was, dead matter. A mechanical object. Like all mechanical objects, he would be dismantled. I laughed at his grimaces.

His penetrable mind was transparent to My gunning vision.

I would murder him. There was simply nothing else to be done.

I had it in mind to pierce the aperture of his penis with a sewing needle.

* *

I trailed endlessly through the streets of Little Poland.

An ineligible bachelor, My "advisor" lived without partners in an amoeba-shaped condominium at the heart of the district, presumably because it is populated by Polish prostitutes and Liechtensteinian transvestites.

LIVE CHICKENS

I slipped into a carniceria, a vacant room reeking of death.

I wanted to inhale the odor of carnage. I wanted to witness the slaughter of powerless animals.

(Parenthetical remark: I once saw Gina Gershon French-kiss a severed boar's head. Dear God or whomever, what will that woman not do?).

Waves of carnage wafted into My nostrils.

A thick layer of liquid faeces lubricated the floor.

A wooden wall partitioned the slaughterhouse from the empty room.

Through a wooden window, I saw an aproned butcher defeathering a chicken. Congealed blood and wisps of plucked feathers coated his butcher's knife.

"You wan' something?"

"No, I just want to watch."

"You can' just stand there. Got to buy something."

"OK, fine. Give Me one white chicken. Throat slit, plucked."

Carmine hens roved across space, their scrawny necks darting out unpredictably.

An effluvium of mist cascaded through the slaughterhouse.

A gaggle of mad chickens packed an undersized coop. Crammed, their heads pressed together.

A black rooster measured Me with stern eyes. Protruding yellow beaks pierced the wire fence. Chicken screeches pierced the rank air.

The Polish butcher pulled a live chicken, fluttering manically, out of the chicken coop. With a gesture exuding the greatest nonchalance, the butcher slit open the chicken's throat. He let the chicken fall.

The chicken sprawled on the slaughterhouse floor.

He pulled the chicken up by its talons and dangled it over a massive steel basin. He dunked the chicken's drooping head into a cylinder that hung over the basin. Purple plasma gushed into the metallic canister and splotched the gray trough below. The blood drained into the drain of the trough.

Quick as speed, the butcher slammed the chicken's body onto a steel table. Drenched with sweat, he hacked off the head and talons of the chicken with a swift knife. Its talons, lacerated, dropped down. Its neck splattered to the floor.

The chicken shivered and then collapsed.

"Pluck?"

"Plucked, yes. I want to watch you pluck the feathers from the chicken."

He began to tear off its feathers.

I jitterbugged out of the butcher's shop with the headless chicken in My arms. I flung the bloodied chicken-corpse into a garbage bin while laughing insanely.

The rank smell of the dead chicken hovered in the alley, which was overlaid with waylaid hoodlums.

A Polish fruit vendor looked at Me with a thick mixture of envy and terror.

FLOATING PAST A CHURCH

I floated past a church.

This isn't heavy-handed symbolism; I did, in fact, float past a church.

There was a Polish wedding. The bridal party paraded out of the doors of the church. Young girls followed the train. Grass sprigs shuddered in the wind.

I shouted to the unexpecting faces of the newly married couple, "Why go to church at all ... when the congregation and ministry are atheists?"

Scorching with white-hot hatred, the Catholic priest spewed violent words.

Whenever I see a Catholic priest, I cringe.

Deep in the shrubbery reclined a child-sized mannequin.

There lay a child, lifeless, without trace of gash or dilaceration. His lips were smoothed by chill evenings, and his eyelids were waxen tulips.

Pray for him, laundrywomen.

Poor stupid child.

No more to do
Now that I am dead
Naked as a fresh fish fillet
In a supermarket

FLASHBACK

My "advisor" once advised Me, "I heard that you applied for a position at Princeton. We'll see how that goes."

He gleamed a toothpasted smile.

Whenever someone says, "We'll see how that goes," this means, "You don't have a chance."

He clawed My arms.

He clamped My shoulders in his lobster grip.

GIRLS IN A CAR SCREAMING CRIES OF DESIRE

I drifted past a restaurant where a pack of geezers devoured their dromedary soup.

A car packed with wild girls sped past Me.

They screamed their cries of desire, "Whore!"

The car was a death barge bucketed by seething harlots. They shrieked and swung their maculate breasts to the air's mandolin. They desired Me, of course, like everyone does. But their desire did not unclothe Me.

Desire reveals nothing but desire itself, chill nothingness.

I AM GOING TO KILL YOU.

Cars flowed down arterial streets like elephantine wanderers crossing glacial frost-lands.

I reached the apartment building of My former "advisor."

An allegedly "attractive" blonde woman in her mid-thirties yanked open the door for Me.

Yes, I *am* the hottest iguana in the reptile house.

She wore a brown suit, I think. It might have been yoke-yellow.

Whenever I flash My eyes, doors unclose.

I frowned at her as I passed. Like everyone else, she felt threatened by Me. Deep inside, she feared My disapproval.

I dove into her watery eyes and swam in the deeps of her aquatic self-hatred.

A swipe of a credit card allowed Me access to his apartment. He hadn't bolted the door.

Beware of beauty. Beauty's a pig, a wanting, a wary sea.

PULLING THE GUN

From the window of his condominium, I saw My "advisor" wheel into the parkway.

He burst out of his automobile, a lime Hyundai, and strode across the tarmac. He tripped over somethingorother and nearly fell into a tree-bin.

I saw Mars, exile planet. Mars resembled a blood bubble, resembled a thought-shroud.

I had a Colt Peacemaker with Me, big as a Big Bertha, packed with slim bullets.

I heard the sound of My "advisor's" footfalls as they ascended the staircase.

My eyebrow follicles stood out. My papillary hair tensed. I heard the sound of a key twisting in a lock.

The lock snapped.

The door swung open, suffusing the condominium with a penumbra of light.

My "advisor" flicked on the light switch, entered, and closed the door.

Our rays of vision crossed. He parted his lips to speak.

"I know why you are here, Mr. Barrows. You feel, wrongly, that I negated your chances of professional success."

My "advisor" sauntered to the kitchenette.

"I contacted the Career Development Center. I know precisely what you did. Debbie made a grave mistake. She won't be getting tenure, that's for sure."

He opened the door of his refrigerator.

"Forgiveness will make you a better person, Mr. Barrows. The doctrine of forgiveness promoted by our founder, Jesus of Nazareth."

Joseph Suglia

He removed a pitcher of water.

"You are cross with me. I can understand why. I could not recommend you with any measure of confidence."

He poured water into a glass.

"It *does* seem that someone with an ego as large as your own wouldn't be well-suited for academe ... Scholarship implies a certain measure of self-sacrifice ... as well as respect for a discipline that is greater than you ... I am *parched*."

He placed the glass to his lips.

"One could express your deficiency in positive terms, of course. You are a self-directed individual. But there are I fear ... certain drawbacks to your fierce individualism. You are far too self-subsistent to be a scholar ..."

He glanced at Me and then turned away, shaking his head as if I were a tiresome little boy.

"This is far too juvenile for you, Mr. Barrows ... Really, these adolescent hijinks ..."

I said nothing, pulled out the Colt Peacemaker from the inside pocket of My tweed jacket, and cocked the hammer.

He stared at Me with befuddlement.

Thick waves of light threw undulating patterns onto his fear-mangled face.

I shoved the revolver close to his right eye.

"What is this about, Mr. Barrows?"

I lowered the barrel of the gun. I jerked the trigger. A ball of fire emitted from the barrel, blasting shattering bone.

His mouth widened to an O. He gasped in the dank air.

"Why?" he mouthed wordlessly.

The bullet struck his right leg — or perhaps it was his left, I can't be sure.

He collapsed to the floor instantly, wringing his limp body with limp hands.

His unclenched fingers clawed traces of pain onto the carpet.

He extended his swelling fingers, seething and cursing inaudibly, the dwarfish man.

Wordlessly, he grasped at My arms. But My arms were not prehensible.

Like a frothing centaur, his mouth gaped, revealing abscesses on his anteater-long tongue — afroth, enraged centaur.

I stepped on his hands and ground them with My steel-toed boots.

I mashed his fingers, Christ-hammering them until the vesicles popped open.

He spat, and his spittle capsized, spiraling back down on his face. Spewing saliva and gnashing his teeth, My "advisor" clawed My trousered legs as I dragged him across the floor.

We reached the bed.

I drew a syringe from My valise.

The syringe ejaculated its juices into his corrugated forehead.

The elephant tranquilizer guaranteed that the mind would be alert, sentenced to a condition of absolute powerlessness.

The eye of the syringe emitted thick dollops of viscous slime.

I administered the marmalade injection, tearing open screaming mouths in the fabric of space-time.

I stuck the needle into his eye-globe in rapid darts.

As he clawed at the air, I pulled out a skein of rope from My valise and wrapped its coils firmly around his

ankles. I bound his hands behind his back with the rope. The lesions on his face crackled and spread open.

He inhaled and exhaled.

⸺ I removed a pair of handcuffs from the valise. Clicking them shut with an audible snap, I manacled his hands with the handcuffs. I arranged his body on the bed, strapping his arms, stretching duct tape tightly over his contorted mouth, duct-taping him fast to the bed.

What was alert was the motor that drove him, his parasite brain.

I tortured My "advisor" while forcing him to be the agog spectator of his own dismemberment.

I unsheathed the revolver, jabbing his forehead with it.

Now reduced to aphasia, he writhed, jerking back and forth like a lobotomized chimpanzee on heroin.

The furrows on his cheeks deepened. The outline of his forehead revealed childhood traumatisms.

I looked into his eyes.

I have never seen such black hatred in the eyes of a human being.

Something persuaded Me to place the gun against his ear.

I teased the barrel of the gun into his aural cavity.

It's so much fun to have complete control over someone else's body.

THE DEFACING

I pulled from My valise a stainless steel battery-operated electric cheese grater. I snapped on the machine. The swiftly rotating blades advanced on his

nose, his cheeks, his eyelids. The blades tore through the duct tape and shredded his lips to bits. The cheese grater collided with his shock-contorted face. A white cloud of minute flesh particles radiated in all directions. The blades sheared free the skin of his face. His non-face resembled a vat of bloody slime. Blood-gelatin gorged his eye-holes. What was left of his face, now unseamed, dropped to the floor, an unused mask.

The electric cheese grater left a ravine where his nose once stood. A gushing geyser of blood fountained from the hole in his face in violent spurts, gushes of thick purple blood. His face was now a filmy silhouette, a tangle of feathery flesh-bits.

I peeled off the necrotic tissue, chipping away, incising, then pulling, skinning off his face, the funny flesh-mask. His white shirt was asmear with purple pig blood; his exposed eyes stared at nothing.

I wanted to cancel them out, those animal eyes.

Hurling My darkling eyes through a shale of tassled hair, I penetrated his elastic mind.

Seized by the giddiness of despair, My "advisor" laughed soundlessly and humorlessly.

In the pelagic depths of his mind stirred unfathomable thoughts. Within his eyes danced the silent agonies of a verbal mind.

His eyes, twin garden eggs.

In his silent mind, he saw his image reflected in the self-reflecting cinema of the self. A shape passed into his thought-vision.

His mind is asizzle with white-hot terror and swarming recollections.

Joseph Suglia

The seams are unstitched; the sutures undo.

THE EMASCULATING

I ensheathed My hands with a pair of transparent surgical gloves.

I unpocketed My switchblade.

Triggered, the blade extruded rudely.

I had it in mind to remove his pudendum, his old man's penis.

I undid the zipper of his blood-stained trousers.

I cut off the button of his trousers with the switchblade.

I ripped down his underwear and yanked out his male organ.

I observed with disgust the reverse heliotropism of the detumescent penis.

Touching this man's genitals suffused Me with thick waves of nausea.

I, at times, despise My flesh but never as strongly as I despise the flesh of others.

I pulled the tip of his penis while hacking away at the base of his genitals with the switchblade.

He screamed. His screams were a stampeding herd of antelope, penetrating rising dust clouds.

My gloves were soon empurpled with blood.

A gluey white film spread over his tongue.

With a sweep of My hand, I ripped free his manhood. As he contorted with pain, I slipped the tip of the lifcless appendage into My "advisor's" lipless mouth.

170

He bit down hard on his penis. His mouth would not accept it. The flesh around the serrated edges of the penis pushed upward, evaginated.

I pinched his nose-flaps.

Clenching his nostrils, I urged the dismembered member into My "advisor's" mouth, which was gagging violently in a frenzy of unimaginable horror. His mouth askew, I shoved the fleshy tube into the deeps of his larynx, dark as a witch's gullet, spearing his throat with the dripping member. Unheeding of his woman's whimperings, I goaded the stringy, testicular mass down his throat. The veins of the half-devoured testicles spooled out of his mouth, gummaceous testicle-veins spooling down his fleshless chin as he vomited streams of black blood.

I refastened the duct tape over his mouthless, skinless mouth, closing the wound.

The striations on his skinless face widened.

Now reduced to a pre-genital creature, My "advisor" possessed a body that was no longer his own, a body marked by creases and folds of My own invention.

At this point, he was faceless and penisless.

A faceless eunuch.

I hacked at your tendons until they ripped open.

I seized, sawed, snatched, gnawed, tearing free your manhood, a mass of dangling tubes, fracturing your flesh, sticking the switchblade into the mouth of your penis, forming a wider hole, while you screeched orangutan-like.

You are a speck of vomit on the carpet of life.

Joseph Suglia

PLAYING WITH THE CAT

My advisor owned a cat named "Richard."

Turning My "advisor" onto his stomach, I scooped up the cat and pushed its head into the hollow of his denuded anus. I urged the cat forward, My hand cradling its furry bottom, as it nuzzled its mouth against the mouth of My "advisor's" rectum.

The cat wormed its flat pink tongue into the orifice.

Using duct tape, I fastened the cat to his hollow anus.

The cat gnawed ravenously at the hole's edges.

The cat chewed away at My former "advisor's" anal cavity.

Goring and burrowing into the opening wound, the cat's head disappeared into the gaping hole.

I did not admire the cat's dank proctophilia.

Braying like a diseased musk ox, the scatoscopophiliac cat seized onto the blood-pink flesh of My "advisor's" rectum.

A thick mixture of phlegm and black blood spewed out of his anus and onto Richard's cat-head.

Coprophile cat.

I drew out an apple corer and an orange reamer from My valise.

I would colostomize My would-be "advisor."

Gripping his blood-matted mane, I cored with the apple corer and reamed with the orange reamer, enlarging the hole of his anus.

Scatophagous cat.

No longer a human being, the being that was once My "advisor" was now a verminous mass, a sexless vermin.

I was not finished with My "advisor."

I drew out a phial from My valise. Within the phial danced wind scorpions.

I inserted the flesh-hungry spiders into his anal aperture.

They would crawl through the tunnels of the lower intestine and devour his colon, liquefying My "advisor's" inner flesh with enzymes secreted from their grinding maws.

A volcanic stream of faeces ruptured out of the aperture, soaking My hands with its excremental flood.

My "advisor" screamed soundlessly.

His cries were a canticle to the sea.

THE ZOOLOGY OF STARS

The elephantine corpse rotted before Me, sodden with blood. His silhouette absented into the damp bed sheets, its surface plasmic and moist with milky spume.

He's dead now, a big flesh-doll.

His dead mouth unleashes an unholy ether.

I plunged the switchblade into his esophagus. I cut free the rope. I cut free the duct tape. He would scream no more.

Unmanacled the garrote around his neck. Unpeeled the duct tape wrapped around his mouth-head.

I sheathed the blade again.

A pre-embryonic state he now is in.

He is not a human being anymore, just a big lumpy flesh-doll lifelessly gargling black blood.

The curtains billow open. I look up at the skies.

The eternal skies are eviscerated. Sidereal blood rains from the heavens.

I see Saturn's frothing rings. The floccus of a dead cloud.

Dead is the sleeping day.

Necro-fields spread across the vast wasteland.

The skies are abubble with black blood.

The skies are asizzle with cosmic effluvia.

The skies reveal inner hair follicles.

Are these the words of a dead man?

Am I dead?

I stare at the skies and catalogue the zoology of stars.

The Crucifixion is the most erotic event in world history.

— Jonathan Barrows

Gretchen Teaches at a High School

I.

Johnny Barrows hates humankind.
No, that isn't quite right.
He is *disinclined* toward human beings.
Hatred, after all, implies love.
And he does not love the other person.
And he does not, then, hate the other person.
The only object of love is the Self.
He has no need of human sociality.
And he loathes cheap sociability.
He exists in a company of one.
He is not a social animal.

Miss Gretchen, the twenty-six-year-old English teacher, should never have disciplined Johnny Barrows. Never, never, never, never. What was he doing in the classroom? Scribbling out a short story or a poem or a philosophy or an ideology or a godknowswhat?
He is a linguistic super-computer, that Johnny Barrows. Even at sixteen, a genius.
She dragged him to the front of the classroom, straight-jacketing his arms with her long fingers.
"Strip!" she cried.
And he refused to strip.
And he refused to lower his monogrammed trousers.
And he refused to reveal the "J.B." that was engraved on his left buttock.
Gretchen unlassoed his belt and pulled down his pants and drawers, disclosing his anus to the

expectant faces of the students. She swung the ruler, emblazoning red stripes on Johnny's beautiful, beautiful white buttocks.

Why did she do this?

In order to properly grasp her reasons, one must have a sense of Gretchen's psycho-sexual history.

Gretchen never dated. Indeed, she avoided members of the opposite gender. The idea of a penis slipping into her vagina filled her with silent horror.

Only once did she extract her secret from the deeps of silence.

She told a priest at confession, "They use that thing to urinate."

Bowing his tortoise-shell glasses, the priest intoned, "I wish that I had three penises ... so that I could invade all of your holes at one time."

That word, *penis* hit her like lightning. Gretchen raced out of the cathedral, her head cradled by clawing hands.

One week later, the priest, who will remain anonymous, committed suicide by shoving the tube of a vacuum cleaner down his throat. Sucking furiously, the vacuum drew out pieces of his liver.

Yes, so intensely ravishing was Gretchen that she inspired her rejectees to kill themselves.

By paddling his bottom, Gretchen released her pent-up sexual frustrations.

Johnny was humiliatingly punished. He suffered long, empty evenings in the Detention Room, where he schematized his revenge — a revenge that was motivated not by hatred, but by necessity.

II.

Though she disciplined them fiercely, Gretchen was well-desired by her charges.

When the woman whom you desire inflicts pain on you, your passion for her intensifies. Every woman knows this. And for this reason, women are painful — painful because they want to be desired.

Johnny played upon the students' sexual sadism. He infused new life into their passion for Gretchen until it fomented into a hissing nest of vipers.

It was a bright autumn afternoon. Light slanted into the cafeteria through beveled windows. Johnny explained to the students that they would have the opportunity to see their teacher naked. Over steaming bowls of Rat Dog Chili, they listened.

"You want to see Miss Gretchen in her natural state, do you not?" Johnny asked.

"Naked, Johnny? We can see Miss Gretchen naked?" Bill Andrews asked, spooning a biteful of octopus calzone into his mouth.

"Yes, you will see her naked."

"All of her? Her titter-tots?" inquired Jenny Traubenwald, itching one of her pubescent nubs.

"Yes, those, you'll see those," Johnny responded.

The students slammed their fists on the table and chanted:

"Ttitter-tots!"

"Jugger-wuggers!"

"Titter-witters!"

Johnny folded his hands and said indulgently, "I have burrowed a hole into the showering area of the girl's lavatory."

The students thundered with approval.

"Keep it down, keep it down!"

Most directed their attention at those heaving mounds of adipose tissue. When she walked, the breasts shivered and shuddered like the snouts of sea lions. Students stared at those massive, jiggling globes as she strode down the hallways of desire.

During English class, the boys and girls would stare gigglingly at the ripe breasts. They fixed their eyes and growled. Gretchen looked at her students with visible embarrassment, trying not to notice their eyes fastened on her delicate nipples. As she grew redder, the nipples grew harder; they pierced the fabric of her cornflower sundress and squirmed beneath the cloth.

After a long day of teaching, Gretchen got herself ready for a shower in the girl's lavatory.

Coach Blumfeld closed off the gymnasium, barricading the entrance.

Gretchen unbuttoned her cornflower blue sundress; the sheath loosened and fell to the tiles. She unhooked her white brassiere; her mesmeric globes flopped out, as white as sandwich spread, her nipples as fresh as the noses of baby opossums. Freed from their velvety prisons, the breasts wobbled and wagged and then settled back into place.

Stepping into the shower stall, Gretchen stretched her arms, her breasts wiggling and wriggling as she walked. Gretchen smothered her hair, menstrual-red, with Banana-Passion Fruit Awareness Shampoo.

She lathered her anus generously with a dollop of Açaí Explosion Moisturizer.

Little did she know that her students were spying on her! Each of those naughty children — Bill Andrews, Jenny Traubenwald, Dan Owen, and Larry Fenton — took turns staring at her silky fat globes, her bucking buttocks and mammary protrusions!

"Milky butterbutt!"

"Slippery butterbutt!"

Johnny seemed strangely unmoved.

How to describe Gretchen's buttocks? Massive, certainly. Absolutely gigantic — definitely. Hilly and fleshy. Yes, yes. Her meaty meat-cups, those undulant pockets of flesh, swayed back and forth as she sashayed down the high school corridors.

Mr. Kraft, the American History instructor, gasped as her buttocks pulsated — rhythmically, musically — grasping them desperately with his thought-vision. He rushed to the lavatory to relieve himself ... wetting his trousers with pre-semen.

Gretchen's buttocks were multi-fissured — traces of cellulite crisscrossed them; otherwise, they were immaculate. The base of her anus was loose and doughy, almost viscous, heavily striated with thick blue veins and fuzzed with light, downy hair. Her natal cleft was profound and served as the "Mason-Dixon Line," as it were, between both protuberant mounds. The contour of her buttocks was dramatic and at the same time flowing. Fluid, fleshy buttocks.

The anal orifice, that gleaming star, was hidden to all — not even she had ever gazed upon it. She wiped the crevasse with moist towelettes. The crease of the orifice was visible through her tight gym shorts. A tuft of reddish-brown hair blossomed like a field of wheat around that aperture, waving waves of anal hair.

So large were her buttocks that Gretchen had a hard time passing through doorways. So large were her buttocks that Gretchen's skirts resembled tents.

The students stared hardly as their teacher moistened the blackish-pink skin of her anal orifice.

"Juicy butterballs!"

"Squishy butterballs!"

She slathered the pendulous breasts with Mango-Cucumber Body Lotion. She clutched and pawed them, shivering like a wallaby in rut, creasing the areolae. They, the areolae, were dark purple and covered with small bumps; the nipples were as white as the breasts. It should also be remarked that the areolae were unusually large — so large, in fact, that they encompassed almost one-third of each breast.

"Look at them titter-tots!" cried Jenny Traubenwald.

Although the breasts were rather tough, the richly textured, saucer-sized areolae were exceptionally sensitive.

Was this the reason that, at the age of twenty-six, she never allowed a man to fondle her precious fruits?

Spumy water cascaded over the breasts; they glistened whitely. She pressed them against her chest and exhaled a dark moan. The nipples rigidified.

Looking down, she exclaimed with distress, "Oh no! There is a hair!"

Indeed, there was a long red hair dangling from the bottom of the manatee-sized right breast.

She tugged furiously at the hair, pulling the breast upward.

She bent her head down and gnashed at the hair with her teeth.

In the darkness of the janitorial closet, Johnny Barrows took a drag of his primrose cigarette and laughed dryly.

The flame of the cigarette formed a glowing red point.

"She's chewing off the titty hair!"

The sight of Gretchen grinding the papillary hair with her teeth threw the students into a frenzy.

Jenny Traubenwald shoved her hand into her skirt and began to manipulate her clitoris until it sprang to attention.

Dan Owen unleashed his penis and massaged its pointy tip.

Larry Fenton rubbed the shaft of his stiffening member.

Bill Andrews dampened his palm with saliva and squeezed his scrotum-sac.

The students stroked their bodies until they fell into exhaustion.

The janitor found them that evening, spent, lying naked in a spreading puddle of semen and vaginal mucous.

Never once did Johnny glance at Gretchen's naked body.

III.

On a bright day in October, Gretchen took the class on a field trip to the arboreal reserve.

She accepted this position only reluctantly, of course; there was simply nothing else to be done. Gretchen was a new teacher, and none of the more seasoned instructors would be hoodwinked into supervising the little daemons.

Her breast-cups bobbed as she ran toward the greenery.

Johnny trailed behind the train.

"Come, students! Come!"

The branches of the white trees shivered against the indifferent sky.

In an infinite expanse of green, they lounged like drunken courtesans, tasting the balmy wind.

Enveloped by meshes of grasses, Gretchen lay down.

The long white tresses of her summer dress caught in the nettles.

A mosquito stung her lithe ankle.

The grass motes undulated slowly.

Gretchen stretched her body across the green.

"Nap time, students!"

They nestled in the nettles, underneath the canopy of leaves.

Gretchen closed her eyes, calmed by the crickets' lullaby.

Pretending to sleep, the students narrowed their eyes.

But the eyes of the students were watchful.

Unclosed.

They were ready.

Johnny whispered, "Do you want to taste her? Yes? Now is your chance. Before you saw her naked. Now you will have her. You will not merely *see*, but *touch* Miss Gretchen's most private areas. You will taste what she tastes like."

Jenny Traubenwald whispered, "I wanna taste Miss Gretchen's honey pot!"

"Soupy, syrupy, pulpy, swampy, pearly, frothy, foamy, gluey, chewy honey pot!"

"Let's lift her skirt!"

As Gretchen snored unmelodically, the children hoisted her skirt, exposing her soft white panties. Jenny Traubenwald ripped them down until they reached her knees. A furry patch, her lovely tuft, was exposed to their vision. Yellow and brown streaks striped her underwear.

"She sure is hairy down there!"

They scythed through the forest of her pubic region with their fingers. They traced the crease of her vulva.

The children were awe-struck.

"Wow! It is beautiful!"

Jenny Traubenwald whispered, "Let me kiss it!"

She bowed her head and kissed the mouth of Gretchen's vagina.

Larry Fenton protruded his tongue and licked the labia majora.

Dan Owen tore a patch of moss from a rock and decorated Gretchen's pubic hair with it.

"Mossy honey pot!"

Brad Wilson dampened his right index finger and penetrated her nether lips, spreading them open with his greedy hands.

Jenny Traubenwald tasted the molasses of her vaginal mucous.

Dan Owen probed his fingers deep into her vaginal canal.

Jenny Traubenwald darted her fingers inside.

"Should we put a frog in there?"

"Or some worms?"

They invaded her dark regions with rude hands, tugging at her tumescent clitoris. They examined her sweet genitals — the gnarls, the lobes, the nodes — rudely palming her pink nether mouth.

Daydreaming, Gretchen imagined foxes licking her vagina.

All of a sudden, she opened her velvet antelope eyes.

The students fell upon her cleft, penetrating it with their greedy excited fingers; their hungry mouths open, they mouthed her womb, sucking the elastic skin of her mons pubis.

Gretchen's large intestine contracted and loosened. Loops of black faeces erupted from her bloated anus,

bursting out violently, rupturing her rectum, shooting out volcanically in all directions, blasting the students with their flailing coils.

A pool of black spread through the meshes of the grasses.

Ladybugs swam in the muddying flood.

The students gorillaed upon her, their eyes burning with lust and rage. They dove, driving her deep into the muddy earth.

Dan Owen and Larry Fenton pinned down her flailing arms. Bill Andrews and Brad Wilson pinned down her fluttering legs. Squatting on Gretchen's stomach, Jenny Traubenwald flung open her instructor's chemise, displaying twin breasts snugly enveloped in a white brassiere, and lifted the cups, revealing the white skin of Gretchen's pert breasts. The white nipples stared at them like helpless eyes. Obscenely large purple discs orbited her straight white nipples, which slowly fossilized until they became as hard as diamonds. She sucked on Gretchen's suckable breasts, pulling on the nipples with her teeth until they smarted and she cried out in pain. As she took fierce draughts from Gretchen's left breast, Larry Fenton seized the base of her right one, waving it back and forth. Gretchen gasped with horror. Larry Fenton played with her right nipple, pinching it until it hardened and spewed forth lactate.

All five of the students gathered around the teacher's exposed breasts and fell upon them, devouring them in a crazed frenzy of sucking and pulling, kneading and massaging, rubbing and fondling, licking and spitting. They wobbled the breasts back and forth, smacking and slapping them, experimenting with them. They measured the breasts,

modeled them, molded them, shaped them with their eager hands.

Jenny Traubenwald lowered her gym shorts and her panties, denuding her anus.

"Let's put the teacher's boob into Jenny's ass!"

"Yeah, let's do it!"

The boys guided Gretchen's right nipple into Jenny's pink anal orifice. The anus eagerly swallowed the tip of the globular breast, which was now covered with the light dust of faecal matter. Jenny bounced up and down, the breast shimmying beneath her weight.

It is difficult for me to conclude this story. I loved Gretchen. I imagined her wriggling breasts coming loose from their brassiere cups, those lacy prisons, size 34DD. I fashioned. I molded. I crafted a wax mannequin in her likeness, an exact figurine, complete with a red mane. Nightly, I permeated the wax mannequin. The hollow between her legs, that delicate fold, is not soft and warm and moist, even though I use corn oil.

A shout from behind.

They turned around to see.

There stood Johnny Barrows.

Stern, implacable.

Gretchen opened her mouth, her eyes wide with horror.

Howling like a daemon, Johnny advanced on Gretchen's screaming skull, slicing the air with a baseball bat spiked with razors and nails.

He hammered down again and again on the sliding slope of what was once her head.

The Intervention of the Third

I.

Io fei giubbetto a me delle mie case.
— Dante Alighieri, *Inferno,* Canto XIII

Andrea and Bobby lounge in the living room, watching *Celebrity Abortions* on television. The reality TV program has millions of viewers worldwide, many of whom dial 1-888-ABORT-IT to cast their vote. Only 38% of the country demanded that Paris Hilton cut short the life of her three-month-old, undifferentiated fetus; the father is rumored to be Orlando Bloom, but Bruce Willis's paternity is also suspected.

Six months have slithered by. Flickering on the cathode ray tube are successive images of Paris Hilton, widening her legs for the camera, wheeled in on a gurney by two sexed-out nurses, the cheeks of their buttocks slightly visible beneath shiny skirts made of polyvinyl chloride. Gripping diamond-studded tongs, his hands ensheathed in surgical gloves, David Hasselhof, the maitre d' of the proceedings, announces gleefully to a thundering audience that "the baby will live!" (the show's slogan and mantra), pulls the caterwauling, slime-glistened mass out of Paris Hilton's bloated vagina, snips the umbilicus with a gigantic pair of steel scissors, and displays the mucous-colored creature to the camera's eye, a burrito of meat, fat, and hair.

Bobby wears a Chick Magnet '65 T-shirt and a pair of blue jeans. His hair is scruffy. He is white, twenty-five-years-old, and unkempt.

Andrea wears a pink sweater and silky pajama bottoms. On her pajamas, alligators play football. Her hair is auburn and bound in a pigtail. She is white, seventeen-years-old, and clean.

Both are sprawled out on the sofa, their arms and legs entangled.

Watching *Celebrity Abortions* was Bobby's idea. A hardened television addict, Bobby once sequestered himself in his single-cell apartment for a week and viewed all two hundred twenty-two episodes of the situation comedy, *Roseanne,* without interruption while devouring the contents of tomato soup cans and smoking marijuana.

Bobby and Andrea have been "dating" — if that is the right word — for five months. They share the following activities — television-watching and fucking. Coitus both optical-aural and vaginal-penile: penetration of the transparent sheet that is the television screen and the penetration of the delicate pink sheath that is Andrea's vulva.

Five months of fucking and television-watching. Instead of looking at each other, they look at the television screen. And then they fuck.

Bobby says little. His gruff nonchalance guarantees his success with members of the opposite gender.

He has fucked Jessica, Jennifer, and Judith — the triad of Andrea's girlfriends.

If he were to express his views on women, none of them would allow him to insert his penis between their legs.

How, then, does Bobby think of women?

Bobby sees women as vulval vehicles, as vectors containing his favorite female body part, the pink crease, the abyssal fold. He has no interest in *women,* strictly speaking; he is only interested in their vaginas.

If there were such things as disembodied vaginas —
warm, moist, and soft — he would purchase them in
bulk.

Andrea does not know this.

Andrea also does not know that Bobby is an
Ovulatory Reductionist.

An Ovulatory Reductionist is one who believes that
women are slaves to their menstrual cycles — that
their behavior is entirely attributable to the flows of
their menstruum.

He also holds that women are prey to the incubatory
impulse — that is, the drive in women to bear
children.

Stretching her supple back, Andrea straightens her
legs across Bobby's groin and eases her cheek gently
against his neck.

She parts her lips to speak.

"Did you hear about that girl on the news? I even
remember her name, Cheryl. That girl got thrown off a
cliff 'cause she blew off a midget."

Bobby looks incredulously at Andrea's bald spot.

"What?"

"Cheryl wrote a book called ... *I Was Thrown from a
Precipice for Sexually Rejecting a Midget.* I think she
was on *Oprah.*"

"What're you talkin' about, Drea?"

"There was, like, this midget and Cheryl blew him
off, and so the midget got revenge by throwing Cheryl
off a cliff."

"Who the fuck is Cheryl?"

"Cheryl is a cheerleader."

"And ... how did you hear about her?"

"On the news."

"And who is ... the midget?"

"The midget was blown off by Cheryl."

Bobby inhales the smoke from his cigarette and stares at its blazing tip. He exhales the smoke through his nostrils like an enraged steer. A shroud of smoke wafts into Andrea's hair.

"Like, I'm telling you, ban cigarettes — and social workers won't have nothing to do. They'll be out of work."

"What are you saying, Bobby?"

Bobby rolls his shoulders, tenses his biceps, and cracks his knuckles.

"It's like ... so many dudes are attracted to nicotine. And social workers get them off the nicotine attraction."

"Isn't that a good thing?"

"Well, yeah, in a way, I guess it is. But think of it this way ..."

Bobby arches his back.

"What happens when there's a cure and people don't need to smoke anymore?"

"There's no more lung cancer?"

"No more lung cancer, yeah, sure, but think of the social workers. Those social workers won't have a job to their names."

"But social workers don't just help people who are attracted to cigarette smoking."

"I'm telling you, Drea, most of what they do is get smokers to stop smoking."

Andrea pauses, looks at Bobby's jeaned crotch, and says, "Makes sense, I guess."

Andrea traces circles on Bobby's left hip and says, "Did I tell you I'm taking a class at the Community College about eco-feminism? Did I tell you about that? The professor is kind of a dork. He's a man-feminist."

"Why is he a dork?"

"I don't know. He has these big glasses and wears purple ties. He's just a dork. But he's taught me all about eco-feminism, and that was cool."

"What is that ... econ-feminism?"

"*Eco*-feminism. It's about helping the environment and helping girls."

"What? I don't get it. How are the two things the same?"

"Well, my professor said that nature is a girl and that we should care for nature 'cause she's a girl. So by saving the baby seals, we're also saving the girls."

Whenever Andrea speaks, she creates landscapes with her voice — hilly hillocks, mountainous peaks, deep ravines, and syrupy brooks. As she speaks, a swamp forms in her speech. Scrawny fins dangle over the shiny black belly of the platypus. A spongy yellow moss coats the limp branch of the yew tree that drops softly into the welcoming swamp. The slimy head of the platypus dunks into the turgid brown water. A drowsy orange cat stealthily insinuates itself through the warped iron gate that borders the swamp. A hippopotamus takes a deep and satisfying shit into its swampy waters.

A qualm stirs within Bobby's scrotum — pressurized semen fomenting like a geyser in a rancid canister of cheese whiz.

Bobby suffers from the super-production of semen in the way that women suffer from yeast infections.

He looks at Andrea meaningfully in the eyes and says, "Wrap your heart in tinfoil, baby, to protect it from the burning flame which is my love."

He sinuates his muscled arm around Andrea's neck, He toys with the cusps of her ears.

Andrea says, bristling, "No, Bobby, I just want to watch TV."

"Come on, give me some of that sweet lovin', girly girl."

"No, Bobby, I don't want to make love right now."

Bobby sighs with exasperation and recoils.

"Whatever."

On the television screen, Angelina Jolie, whose labial sphincter approximates the span of her genital lips, squirms and cries, "My baby! My baby!"

Her head resembles a skull covered in a white curtain.

She thrashes and writhes on a gurney, strapped down by the two sexed-out nurses. A close-up of her furry pudenda fills the screen. Angelina Jolie's vaginal fissure has never before been seen in public, save *via* the bootleg version of *Taking Lives* (2004), transferred from Japanese laser disc.

Using a turkey baster, David Hasselhof injects a jet of methotrexate into Angelina Jolie's genital canal while a nation thunders with applause.

Andrea is asleep. She snores uncontentedly. She misses the spectacle that unfolds on the television screen.

Bobby, newly enthralled, is infused with lust by the sight of Angelina Jolie's exposed nether parts. His eyes crazed with neon, Bobby presses his hands underneath Andrea's pink sweater and grips and palms her soft white bulbs, bobbing them up and down. He massages his fossilizing penis while teasing the tear-drop nipple of each breast.

Manipulating her nipples, Bobby whispers to himself, "Put it in Cool Control, and gear it into Cool Mode, because we are entering the Cool Zone."

Softly, stealthily, Bobby lowers Andrea's pajamas from behind, inching them down, parting the cheeks of her succulent buttocks. He exposes the ridged star of her anal orifice and probes its edges, fingering her rectal region.

Bobby's tongue snakes through his lips.

It is the protrusible tongue of the aardvark.

He sticks his tongue into the pink star of her buttocks.

He splits the cheeks of her anus and spits inside.

Spittle drops from his tongue into the deep crevice.

He wags his penis until viscous goo oozes from its aperture.

Spewing semen cascades into the cleft of Andrea's buttocks, dripping from its hardened tip.

II.

The mentally feeble, when confronted by a man of greatness, give rein to their envy, self-hatred, and stupidity.

— Jonathan Barrows

Squatting on the sofa, Bobby pulls off his socks. On television is *Meatballs, Part Five: Back to Camp!* (2005), starring Bobcat Goldthwait and Leslie Easterbrook as aging summer-camp counselors who are stripped naked, flagellated, and crucified by the campers under their charge.

Balancing on the parapet of the camp fortress, Leslie Easterbrook, her mammothine breasts swaying underneath a translucent nightgown, screams at the brigade below, "You teenage dirtbags! You teenage dirtbags!"

The fortress smolders and sinks.

"I used to be a teenage dirtbag," Bobby says unyoungly. "Now, I'm just a dirtbag."

With a fistful of tissue paper, that universal blotter of excrement and semen, Bobby erases the lineaments of his seminal fluid from the anal rift of his involuntary lover.

"Let me bless you with my jiz ... Hey, Drea! Wake up, babe!"

"Hum?"

"Wake up, bitch!"

Bobby snickers to himself.

Her face pressed into a mucous-splotched pillow, Andrea swivels her body and asks, "Whaaat? What you say?"

"I said, 'Wake up, Drea!'"

Puzzledly, Andrea hoists her pajama bottoms and places her feet on the thorny carpet.

"Drea!" Bobby exclaims over-loudly.

"Bobby, what is it? What is so urgent?"

"That kid you're babysitting. Where is he?"

"Johnny? Upstairs ... I think."

"What if he saw us?"

"Saw us do what?"

"Saw us ... make out."

"Saw us make out? Bobby, what are you ...?"

"We made out a little while ago, right?"

"Yeah ...?"

"Well, you're seventeen, and I don't want his parents to know about that shit."

"Bobby, it's not against the law to kiss a seventeen-year-old girl."

"Look, I just don't want the Barrows to know that we've been fooling around and shit."

"They're not going to know. They're away for the whole week in Norwegia and Dutchmark."

"What's that kid's deal, anyway? Doesn't he, like, ever leave his room?"

"No, I've only seen him outside of his bedroom once or twice."

"How old is he?"

"He's thirteen."

"And you're only four years older than him? And you're his babysitter? Man, that is so fucking hot."

"He's really cute ... for a kid, I mean."

"I'll bet he'd love to jiz up your nose and shit."

"That's gross."

"Well, I bet he would ... like to slide it in ... right to the top."

"No, he doesn't like girls."

"What, like, he's a faggot or something?"

"No, he's not really into boys either. At least that's what his sister said."

Bobby taps his cigarette into a porcelain ashtray and asks, "What the fuck does that mean? So, like, he's not into girls. And he's not into boys. So what is he, a sheep-fucker?"

"No, he's in love with himself."

"Huh? I mean, what?"

"He's got a crush on himself."

"What?"

Bobby presses a glass of Tang to his lips and takes a swig, which gives to his palette a tangy tingle.

Andrea say, "He makes himself hard."

"What ...?"

"He has naked pictures of himself and gets off on them."

"Wait ... Wait ... Hold up ..."

"That's why there's jiz all over the house, Bobby. He jizzes on the walls and stuff while looking at pictures of his dick."

Bobby probes his ear canal with his right index finger, excises a quantum of wax, and studies the shapeless yellow mass as if it were a vital natural resource.

He asks, "Does he anal himself too?"

"Bobby, I don't know."

"Does he, like ... Wait. Does he, like, lick his own cock and drink his own jiz?"

"I don't know. His sister didn't say."

Bobby stares at the mobile castle of Andrea's breasts, those bouncing mountains, a mountaineer surveying the valley that divides them.

Oblivious of his gaze, Andrea asks Bobby softly, "Bobby ... Did you ever, like, want to shave off all of your hair?"

"Shave off all of my hair?"

"Yeah, shave it all off. Not just your hair on your head, but your eyebrow hair and eyelashes and the hair on your pubes and the hair on your ass and your ear hair and your armpit hair and stuff ..."

* * *

Gentle Reader, I must interrupt my story at this point. You are probably wondering why I've entitled this composition, "The Intervention of the Third." Let me explain.

Every "normal" relationship is a *triangulated* relationship.

Whenever two heterosexuals connect, there is always the intervention of "the Third" — that is to say, the stranger, the pervert, the Peeping Thomas, the ex-

boyfriend, the stalker, the homosexual, the auto-eroticist, the witness, the Intermediary, He-Who-Should-Not-Be-There.

What have you.

Of whom do lovers talk?

Of perverts.

Of lovers past.

Of whom do lovers think as they lie in their beds?

The Third. Yes, the Third invades the space of your relationship. Indeed, without the Third, you would have no relationship.

Young maid, when you couple with your boyfriend in the privacy of your parents' Sports Utility Vehicle, clutch his shoulders, and mix your saliva with his, do not think that you are alone.

You are not alone. The Third is watching you.

And when you tear off your egg-colored brassiere and show your boyfriend the nubs of your ovoid breasts, those hard pink tips standing out like pencil erasers, do not imagine that you are alone.

The Third is watching you.

The Third comes before the First and the Second.

Without the Third, there would be no heterosexuality. Without the Third, there would be no congress between erotic counterparts, no sexual partnerships at all. No one would be able to relate to the other without the intervention of the Third.

You mustn't misunderstand me. I am not suggesting that Jonathan Barrows is a voyeur. (Yes, he did watch Bobby spit his saliva into Andrea's anal orifice and ejaculate on her ripe young buttocks.)

Jonathan Barrows derived no pleasure whatsoever from the viewing of this act.

What I am suggesting is as follows: Andrea and Bobby are deeply preoccupied with Jonathan Barrows.

Jonathan Barrows is the Third.

Without the possibility of his presence, their bodies would never fuse together.

Meaning does not take place in isolation.

* * *

"Let's see if we can break him in. Come on!"

Bobby and Andrea bound up the staircase, gearing toward Johnny's bedroom.

Bursting into the sanctuary of his enclosure (these are the days before the door was sealed with a lock), Bobby pinions Johnny's arms behind his back, disabling him as he squirms for liberty. Her teeth ablaze, Andrea rips down Johnny's sweatpants, denuding his penis, which stares at her with its venomous mouth.

Johnny hisses with devil rage, a rage so intense, so black, so vile, so unearthly that Bobby loosens his grip and stands back, shivering.

Andrea shrinks back, arching her head, looking up at her God-Daemon, whose eyes are burning blackly, comets of hatred.

He widens his jaw and screeches a shattering screech.

"What the fuck?"

"Johnny, we're only playing around!"

Quivering with animal fear, Bobby and Andrea retract into the darkness of the room.

Andrea and Bobby will know the limits of pain.

They will be strung up like sausages in a meat locker.

They will be tortured like thrashing embryos.

III.

Or discendiamo omai maggior pièta;
già ogni stella cade che saliva
quand' io mi mossi, e 'l troppo star si vieta.
— Dante Alighieri, *Inferno,* Canto VII

Lust is the destroyer of patience.
— Jonathan Barrows

Johnny crumbles off a bit of oatmeal cake and feeds it to the freak. When it opens its mouth, you hear the sound of a vacuum, of the wind echoing through an infinite abyss.

The freak is composed of two bodies stitched together with black wire — that of she who was once called "Andrea" and that of he who was once called "Bobby." Both shapes have formed, melded, coalesced into a single physicality, a hairless, formless white mass that resembles a gigantic, writhing larva or the single white tentacle of a hydra. It stretches its suckers around buzzing cockroaches, trying to capture them in the hives of its mouths.

"Bobby's" penis was severed from his body last week — and one could say that the freak resembles, not merely a larva or a hydra's tentacle, but also a massive, disembodied male genital organ. It slithers across the wooden planks of the floor in the abandoned, ramshackle cabin.

Looking into the eyes of the freak is like looking into the eyes of a chicken: there is only null, blank space to be seen.

Johnny tears off another piece of the oatmeal cake and lowers it into the androgyne's more feminine

Joseph Suglia

mouth, which is puckered like the mouth of a puffer fish. The freak's naked white teeth and gums are wholly exposed. Lipless thing. While it was slumbering (under the influence of a bull tranquilizer), Johnny carved ovals around the freak's mouths with a sharp hunting knife. The knife cut deeply, creating fleshy wattles around the holes. *Blood saturating the wooden floorboards.* He carved free its lips and stuffed the bloody ribbons of flesh down the freak's throats. He extirpated the tongues, the roots of which are now loose polyps of flesh lolling around in the freak's mouths.

The freak is without appendages. Johnny shaped its body with the hunting knife, amputating the arms and the legs. He cauterized the wounds with an acetylene blowtorch.

The freak is sterilized, completely white, and naked. Dripping with bloody dew, Johnny sheared off the freak's hair using an electrical razor.

What Johnny did was not cruel, but rather the logical extension of the lovers' attitudes.

Only the moon gives light to the shapes in the cabin. As the moonlight cascades into the main room of the cabin, the columns cast shadows across the floor. The freak is a slippery, quivering mass of gelatin, shivering and moist. The creased skin of the freak resembles peeling wallpaper — fleshy squid of alabaster skin.

Now alert and yet as senseless as a fish, the freak flaps its arm stubs as if they were flippers.

On the portable radio, Larry Lewandowski sings:

My hair's so greasy you can call me slick.
My balls're so big you can bowl wit' 'm.

Crumbling off pieces of the cake, Johnny circles the freak, feeding it particles of oatmeal in the abandoned, ramshackle cabin in the forest.

He gazes at the thing before him, a pillar of succulent, wet flesh littered with bumps, nodes, and excrescences.

Johnny says, "You are copious self-hatred become man."

There is a practice popularized by Richard Gere known as "gerbilization." Bluntly stated, this implies the insertion of a gerbil into the anus of a patient. The veterinarian de-claws the gerbil; she then excises the teeth and greases its body with lard. She fastens a tube to the patient's anus with duct tape. The tube must be well-lubricated. The body of the patient is positioned prostrate upon the veterinarian's table. Placed within a Ziploc bag, the gerbil is shot through the slick tube. The gerbil squirms and fidgets within the patient's colon. The squirming and fidgeting of the gerbil produces an erogenous effect within the patient. The veterinarian pulls the gerbil out by its tail. It is important that the tail not snap.

On the third day, Johnny gerbilized Andrea, sticking a live hamster into the dry space of her vagina. The hamster was not sheathed in a Ziploc bag. Nor was it de-clawed.

The hamster scurried down the tunnel, gnawing her insides until it burrowed its way into her rectal cavity.

Black goo spills out of the freak's mouths.

Watch the freak ooze across the planks on the floor.

The rodent is still alive inside of the freak. It will devour the freak from the inside out.

Lightless dungeon now.

"My mind's clean of you," Johnny says.

To love someone is to want to become him. And did Andrea and Bobby not achieve every lover's goal? They fused together into a single body — the impossible objective of everyone who desires.

Without the intervention of the Third, there is no synthesis.

Without the intervention of the Third, there is no love.

Without the intervention of the Third, there is no desire.

Without the intervention of the Third, the One cannot relate to the Other.

Soon, the freak will collapse lifelessly into the shadows.

Let the dead fuck the dead.

Project for the Assassination of X.

I am devouring a cheeseburger. Two leaves of lettuce, a tomato slice, and a spider web of mayonnaise, mustard, and ketchup make up the first level of the three-tiered cheeseburger structure. The tomato slice is succulent and rich, flavorful and greenishly overripe. The leaves that umbrella the tomato are overly crisp; I prefer the lettuce on My cheeseburger to be moist and flimsy. A ribbon of mustard, mayonnaise, and ketchup wettens the hoods of the lettuce leaves. A multitude of sesame seeds pock the dome of the cheeseburger roll; its underside is slightly browned and littered with the mayonnaise curls, the mustard trails, and the ketchup spirals. Upon the leaves, the ketchup, the mustard, and the mayonnaise are bleeding together in a liquid swirl. There is, perhaps, too much egg and milk in the dollops of mayonnaise that splotch the underside of the upper bun and douse the hoods of the lettuce leaves. Beneath this tangle of condiments and vegetables lies a trapezoid of orange cheese, resting upon the patty of beef, which is richly textured, of a complex consistency, and brownish-black with translucent pockets of fat — My teeth can make out the traces of fat and bone that have not yet been assimilated into the wad of flesh. I moisten My tongue. Stuffing the mass into My mouth, I swallow a clump of brownish-black beef, a triangle of cheese, an eely coil of tomato, and a thatch of lettuce — all of which are dampened by mustard, mayonnaise, and ketchup.

Strapped to a chair in front of Me is the world's most celebrated pop diva. I am sitting across from her,

a rifle lying horizontally across My thighs. She hardly looks like a celebrity at all. An ordinary she-creature, an intermediate, shadowy half-form, neither girl nor woman, a youngish woman, a womanish girl, whimpering. Her eyes are so wide, you'd think I had ripped her eyelids off — which I haven't done.

I trailed her in the nightclub, seduced her, led her away from the entourage of bouncers, stylists, lawyers, and publicists that surrounded her ("He's cool. Don't worry. I'll call y'all later") — after all, I am handsome and therefore harmless. She speaks with a Southern twang. Once we reached the parking garage of My apartment building, I drugged her, dragged her into the freight elevator, and stowed her in My loft. She is conscious now, duct-taped to the chair, half-choking on the ball gag I inserted into her mouth.

On the radio is her new single, "Funkalicious," from the album of the same title.

We're moving it up
And we're moving it down
We move it to the city
Then we move it uptown
We're moving it up
Where the party people go
Go fresh, Funky Daddy
Funky Daddy, make it flow

Flow, flow
Watch me flow
Some take it fast
Some take it slow

We walk in the club
My girls and me

There are boys all around
Shakin' their butts
Some boy comes up to me
He grabs my waist
Then we start to dance
All over the place

Funkalicious
Fantastic
I'm the girl with all the plastic

Funkalicious
Fantastic
I'm the girl with all the plastic

Boys uptown
Do it like you should
Everyone is prey
To my funkalicious ways

She is by no means unintelligent. (Studying the loft up and down, her lidless eyes trace outlines.) Television would present her that way, as if intelligence were incompatible with the pleasantness of the flesh. What she is, is ordinary — fascinating in her ordinariness, in her banality, in her everydayness — she, interchangeable with any other twenty-three-year old American girl. There is absolutely nothing remarkable about her.

How is one to explain the fact that this girl is one of the most recognized figures in Western culture?

She is emblematic of what one might call "the Carson Daley concept of fame": the less distinctive you are, *the more likely you are to become famous.*

Joseph Suglia

The standards of prestige have been liquefied. Prestige is no longer based on talent or effort or even beauty, but rather chance.

Prestige is disorganized misunderstanding.

To say, "Anyone can be famous" may seem banal — and yet it is nonetheless true.

A man who is attacked by a tiger in a zoological garden may become famous.

Celebrity is absolutely exchangeable.

She is not even particularly beautiful, imaginative, or amusing.

She is not famous *despite* her ordinariness. She is famous *by virtue of* her ordinariness.

She is absolutely indistinguishable from "the average girl" — and *therefore* is one of the most famous pop stars in Western civilization.

Literally anyone in this culture may be elevated to the status of godhood. If all of the old gods are dead, as we are told, the new gods are celebrities. Their love affairs, their politics, their inclinations — all of these trivialities are objects of obsession.

Television sinks the spectator into his own insignificance.

His god is the twenty-three-year-old girl-woman with glycerine-lubricated gums. He takes malicious satisfaction in the failings and shortcomings of the celebrity. The spectator is envious, mired in his self-hatred, conscious of his worthlessness.

Television is pure transcendence.

My decision to assassinate her was not provoked by hatred.

Every human being desires desire, perhaps is nothing else but the desire to be desired.

The one who is filmed is desired. To be filmed is to be desired. To be desired by everyone is to become god.

Television is the apotheosis of experience.

The New God is the Celebrity. The Celebrity is the New God.

Instead of looking at each other, we are trained to look at the stars.

* * * * * * * * * * * * * * * * * * * *

Leaning against the balustrade, I load My rifle. Everywhere declines the declining day. Zigzags of light play on the barrel. From the balcony, I watch a homeless man masturbate in the alley. He ejaculates on a rat. *Let me christen you with my semen.* Droplets of white fluid cling to the rat's fur.

"Jesus is gonna open up a can of whoop-ass."

That is what she said to Me before I gagged her.

"Words cannot describe how stupid you are."

I rummage through My toolbox and pull out a pair of electric hedge clippers. I advance upon My Cinderella, writhing and twitching in horror. I slide off the shoe on her right foot. I hold the heel of the right foot in My hands. It is unusually large for such a small girl. Bluish veins stand out through translucent skin. Each toe is painted a different color, which gives to the entire foot the grotesque appearance of a circus. The sole is well-scrubbed and faintly perfumed; it is solid, whereas the rest of the foot seems somewhat delicate. There is not a trace of hair on any of the digits. The toenails are finely manicured — each one forms a crescent. Between the toes are folds of webbed skin, completely absent of toe lint. I manipulate the toes with My fingers — they draw back, as if retracting into their shell, as if they knew that each one would soon be severed from the base of the foot.

"This little piggy went to market."

I place the blades of the hedge clippers around the big toe. Color: Santa's Candy. I press the handles together, and the blades close, slicing through the shield of skin and muscles. The elastic skin recedes, but the bone is stubborn. I close down upon the toe again, but the phalanx will not yield, hanging from a stalk of bone, muscle, and tendon. I exert more strength and drive together the handles. The maws of the clippers bite down harder, and the big toe yields, dropping to the floor with an audible splash, immersed in a cascade of purple blood.

"This little piggy stayed home."

A single sweep of the blades releases the second toe from the foot. Color: Breezy Beach. The wormy toe sticks to the clippers. Streams of blood run down the blades.

"This little piggy had roast beef."

The middle toe of the right foot is rabbity — it writhes, it twitches, it turns. Color: Strawberry Sorbet. I twist it around, pulling the toe back until the nail reaches the midfoot. I hear the snap. I seize a hunting knife, drawing it out of the toolbox. I free the limp appendage from her body and fling it across the room; the toe splatters against a wall and falls squishily to the ground.

"This little piggy had none."

The fourth toe resembles a sea lamprey's tail. Color: Fruit Sangria. I hack away at the bone with the hunting knife, which loosens the toe nicely. I pull on that toe until it detaches from the foot.

"This little piggy said, *Weeeeeeeeeeeeee* ... all the way home!"

The blade descends on the little toe and frees it. Clean and easy. Color: Plumberry Crumb.

* * * * * * * * * * * * * * * * * * *

"Do you like water sports? I do water sports. Just like Marilyn Monroe."

She rubs her clitoris.

"Set me free, and I'll do whatever you want."

Her mouth is slippery with vomit.

"I'll drink my own pee."

She is sobbing now.

I am burning thoughts in the furnace of her mind. On the balcony, I weigh the rifle in My strong hands. Urinating against the wall, the homeless man roars like a leopard.

I saw her once dining on grasshoppers in red chili at a fashionable Hollywood restaurant. Will her toes taste the same way?

Her words filling her mouth with pain. The twisting of her body — the writhing, the twitching. She struggles with the bonds.

My eyes pierce her own, eyes that seem to be without lids.

I'll force her to eat her own toes too.

I will cut off one of her breasts, fasten it to a stick, and whip her with it.

* * * * * * * * * * * * * * * * * * *

Patterns of blue lights flash in the darkness of the interior. Police cars snake around the apartment building. Soon will come the clatter of footfalls down the corridor, the booming of reports after they batter-ram open the door.

Not before I shoot her head off.

Stepping into the lavatory, I unlasso My belt and lower My trousers.

Squatting on the toilet seat, I sigh unmelodically.

My colon loosens and contracts.

A geyser of faeces blasts out of My anus, moving through space at supersonic speeds, spraying its shimmering trails in all directions like a supernova.

Winds of black, spiralline, propulsively emanating from My insides.

Listen to My creamy faeces as it sloshes into the foam.

About the Author

Joseph Suglia earned a Ph.D. in Comparative Literary Studies at Northwestern University. His other books include *Hölderlin and Blanchot on Self-Sacrifice* and *Years of Rage.* What will become of him is anyone's guess.

935252

Made in the USA